# GHOST CAVE MOUNTAIN

By

Karen J Simon

# GHOST CAVE MOUNTAIN

Copyright ©2012 by Karen J. Simon
Cover Artwork ©2012 by Karen J. Simon

Published by:
Alaska Dreams Publishing
P.O. Box 72156
Fairbanks, Alaska 99707
www.alaskadp.com

Revised 8/22/12

ISBN numbers:
ISBN-13: 978-0-9855588-4-0
ISBN-10: 0985558849

Also by
KAREN SIMON:

# INSIDE THE CIRCLE

*"One Woman's Search for the*
*Cause of the Violence that Tore Apart a*
*Family and Destroyed a Marriage"*

Kindle E-Book & Print version available at:
www.amazon.com

Nook E-Book version available at:
www.bn.com

Karen J. Simon

# TABLE OF CONTENTS

Karen J. Simon

# DEDICATION

From the time we are very young, there are people who have some influence in guiding us - be they family members, friends, teachers, co-workers, pastors, or civic leaders, authors, poets and artists There are people who touch our lives by example, some who say only a few words that seem to echo down the halls of time, and some we never meet influence us only because we sat down and read what they had written or admired what they had created. Whether we remember the people or not, whether we recall certain incidents or not, whether we remember the name of the book or author matters not; what they have imparted stays with us. They have all become a part of the fabric of our own life – the ghosts of our past. This book is dedicated to all those who have, by example or word, affected my life, guided me – whether seen or unseen, known or unknown.

Karen J. Simon

# ACKNOWLEDGEMENTS

Many have encouraged me to write, to paint, to create. And many have had patience while I put life – and them – on hold while I finished one more paragraph, added one more detail to a painting or finished one more step on a sewing or beading project.

My son, Rodney – "Where are you, mother, we've been ready to go for fifteen minutes."

My granddaughter, Ariel – "Gramma! Come on! I'm waiting!"

And those who encouraged:

My boss – Barbara – "You should publish it, Karen."

My friend, Darlene – "Way to go, Karen!"

My ex-boss, Jay – "You're wasting your talents working here."

My neighbor and friend – Brenda – who has sat quietly and patiently and listened to every word; giving criticism and advise, noting misspelled words, punctuation, roughly written phrases or areas that called for more clarification.

My publisher who has guided and encouraged all of my efforts.

I thank all of you – without your encouragement and support I wouldn't be writing this.

Karen J. Simon

# CHAPTER 1

A thin band of light haloed the top of the mountain where the sun had disappeared as a slender figure stepped from the darkness of the trees along the old logging road. She braced her body as she slid down the steep slope to the road itself, then stood straight to look first up the road and then down to get her bearings. She readjusted the straps of her backpack, brushed a hand across her forehead and tucked a stray strand of red hair back under the faded blue baseball cap and turned to walk down the road. Light was fading fast and the battered old truck was parked a good half mile below her, backed into an overgrown dead end fork in the road.

That old black truck, a box of yellowed papers and a lifetime of stories about this mountain were all that were left of her father. She had spent the better part of the last two years searching this mountain for some clue to her father's disappearance. The old truck had been found further up the mountain on a side trail, but a winter avalanche had blocked access to that area the winter after her father disappeared.

She had just started working for the Forest Service, was preparing to go out on her first fire watch tower when her mother called. The Service had allowed her an extension of leave and then she had begged for a transfer to this area after all hope had been abandoned.

Andrew John McDougal was a quiet teacher of history with a passion for the outdoors and ancient culture. The pristine mountains of northern Idaho had given him a veritable open door to a wilderness little touched by the hand of man. Drawn by the history of gold in the territorial days, he had settled his wife and daughter in a small town nestled at the base of the towering Rockies. Though his winters were dedicated to his students and the classroom, his summers were soon dedicated to working for the Forest Service, giving him the opportunity to wander, explore and camp in the mountains that were his new back yard.

Every area touched by gold fever had its legends of lost gold mines, lost gold shipments and lost miners. The mountains bred tales of Big Foot, lost Indian tribes, old battle grounds, missionaries, fur traders, early explorers, rendezvous, trading posts, ghost towns, old forts, and early settlers passing through. Andrew was fascinated by all of the stories. He tracked them down, researched them and wrote them out in his own hand. His favorites became bedtime stories when Andrew was home long enough to spend time with his only child.

It was not unusual for him to be gone for weeks during the summer, whether it was work or pleasure. In her teens, Natalie had talked him into taking her on camping and exploration trips and he had eagerly taken her to the site of old logging camps, ghost towns, trading posts and rendezvous. For the most part, little remained of the activity that had created them in the first place, but here and there some remnant had survived the ravages of time, weather, fires and man. A few buildings in various stages of collapse, a board, a roughhewn log that might have been part of a building, a jumble of rock to mark the location of fireplaces and chimneys overgrown by grass and brush. Trees and rocks bore the marks of knife or ax – initials, stick figures, crosses, arrows, names, hearts or simply just slashes or notches. In some locations Andrew had left his own cache of items he had found somewhere in the vicinity – a broken jar, an old metal can, a rusted gold pan, a piece of broken pottery, a hand full of arrow heads, a few rounds of old lead shot, colored trade beads, chunks of quartz, an empty shell casing, brass buttons, part of a shell comb and bits and pieces of broken colored glass, shells and bones. He had told her the story of each find and together they had discussed the possibilities surrounding each item. From him, she had seen the world through different eyes, revisited the past as if it were only yesterday and learned to love the land, the mountain and its past as few others had bothered.

Little wonder that she had gravitated to the same interest and had chosen archeology as her college major with forestry as a minor. They revisited some of the sites and even added a few more artifacts to the caches – a small shard of an old mirror, a piece of harness leather attached to a rusted iron ring, a few rusty nails, more arrow heads and a small dark blue bottle. They never thought to take the items home, for there they had no value. Left alone, they told a story of life where they were found. Location of items and caches were carefully noted in both written notes and hand drawn maps. A 'C' accompanied by a number was traced on a terrain map and a note in the margin at the bottom referred to the written notes for more information regarding the site.

Then in June, two years before, her father had gone out camping for a few days. After a week, his wife had become worried and called the Forest Service. Another week passed before Natalie was called and a search began in earnest. Andrew's truck had been found parked on an old logging road on the mountain. No trace of Andrew or his camping gear was ever found. Lettie McDougal explained that her husband had just obtained several new terrain maps to take with him and had taken enough supplies to last a good week and several days.

Natalie had combed through her father's notes and maps looking for some clue as to where he might have gone. She led search parties to each site and they scoured the areas with no success. Search parties radiated out for miles using the truck as the center of the search grid. Helicopters had gone up and down the mountain, skirting the ridges at tree line, barely skimming tree tops as their rotors beat the air above. Weather had been good for most of the time; blue cloudless skies, scattered afternoon and evening thunder storms, but nothing major that would have created a danger for campers, boaters, hikers or climbers.

Sheriff Chester Greer sat down with Natalie and her mother and asked for a detailed list of items that Andrew had taken with him. After going over the list they decided that he would have had to make two or three trips to the truck to take all of his supplies in. Natalie related that she and her father had used old sites as staging points to cache supplies when they went on extended camping trips, but no sign of recent disturbance had been found at the sites to indicate that her father had stopped at any of them. Her father had parked the truck and simply vanished with all his camping supplies and the search was abandoned after he had been gone for a month. Two years and the mountain kept its secret.

The Forest Service had allowed Natalie to attach to a fire fighting unit out of Missoula, Montana in late July. It was close enough for her to be home on weekends with her mother and close enough for her to continue to search the mountain. Late last winter, an office position opened at the park here and she had snapped the offer up.

Natalie shrugged out of her backpack and threw it onto the truck seat. She climbed in after it, closed the door and turned the key in the ignition. The headlights probed the gathering darkness as she maneuvered slowly down the narrow winding passage that was all that remained of the old logging road. By the time she turned onto the main road, stars glittered in the sky above and a half moon peeped through a vapor thin cloud. A set of tail lights blinked ahead of her, but other than that, the road was deserted until she turned onto the highway just outside of town. The weekend campers and hikers had already long headed for home and few lived on the stretch of road that led into the lower park.

Just about a quarter mile out of town, she turned onto a secondary road and then turned into the third road on the right. A canopy of branches cast dappled patterns of moonlight across the surface of the ground as the truck wound through a small grove of trees. Then a security light popped on as the truck passed the front gate, flooding the yard with its bright glow.

Natalie parked the truck in front of the garage, scooped up her backpack and hurried to the back door. As her foot landed on the bottom step, the back porch light came on and the door opened.

"Mmmmmm. Whatever it is, it smells good, Mom." Natalie dropped her backpack, settled her cap on it and ran her fingers through her hair.

"Meat loaf pie, fresh biscuits and apple cobbler. I'll set you a place while you wash up. Do you want milk or iced tea?"

"Iced tea. Please! It was hot out there today." Natalie splashed water on her face in the half bath just off the kitchen.

When she returned, a steaming plate of food was on the table with two tall glasses of iced tea. Lettie set two smalls bowls of hot apple cobbler on the table and sat down.

Natalie knew what her mother wanted, but she ate in silence until her mother spoke.

"Anna called today."

"What's new in Augusta?"

"Anna wants me to visit."

"And?"

"She thinks I should stay – at least for the winter – maybe think about staying longer."

"That's your decision, Mom, but I don't think the vacation part is a bad idea. You haven't been back since Gran passed away and that was about five years ago, if I recall correctly. You and Anna have always been rather close, too, haven't you?"

"I'm just not sure anymore, honey. I…………" her voice trailed off as she looked toward the window above the sink.

"I know, Mom. But it's been two years. I keep going over the same ground. I just don't see anything and I keep thinking there should be something. I know you want closure as much as I do. After all this time, I still almost expect to walk into one of the sites and find him digging something new out of the ground and asking what took me so long to get there. As long as I live here, I'll keep going to the mountain and as long as I keep going to the mountain, I'll keep looking….hoping. The last time you went home, everyone was grieving the loss of Gran; you didn't have time to really enjoy the people, the places. You need to find life again, Mom, stay with Aunt Anna. Visit Uncle Bert. Look up old friends. Enjoy some time away. There's really nothing here for you, Mom. All of your family is in Augusta. Maybe moving back will appeal to you once you have experienced it again. And that's OK."

"You're here. And your father…"

"Dad's not really here anymore, Mom, and my job could move me out of here, you know that. At some point, someone above me will say the same thing to me – 'move on' and I may have no choice.

17

Then you'll be here alone. Where ever you are, I can visit, too. Call Aunt Anna and tell her yes, then start looking at flights and packing a couple of bags. From there, we'll just take one step at a time."

# CHAPTER 2

The air conditioning unit in the office quit working just after lunch on Friday and there would be no one to look at it before Monday. Natalie opened the windows and the front door, but the air outside was as calm and hot as that inside. She sipped ice water from a Styrofoam cup and picked up a packet of papers - last weekend's park visitor counts and camp receipts. The last of them were entered into the computer data file, she just needed to make sure everything was accounted for before printing a copy of the report to file with the receipts.

"Hey! In case you hadn't noticed, it's hot enough to fry eggs on the sidewalk. Lovin nature is one thing, but girl, turn the AC on before you cook!" Kevin Blair, the park supervisor and her boss, dropped his hat on the counter and wiped sweat from his forehead. "This heat keeps up; we're apt to be in for some fires. Have the PE crews checked in yet?"

"Bear Paw Creek lot has two spots left. Lower Falls Road has a good dozen, but it'll probably fill before the end of the day. Two Dice and Quincy Road have very few and I haven't heard from Logan Bench and Trail Head. Upper Falls and both lots at

Quarter Horse are still closed. And the AC won't get fixed until Monday at the earliest."

"Do you want to go ahead home for the weekend? Forward the phone and let Stan and the guys handle any more calls down at the call center. It's just way too hot to be inside in this heat with no air."

"Let me finish this report and I'll close up. Thanks Kev."

"Excuse me, please, but where could I find Lee McDougal?"

"You found her." Kevin announced as he passed the man just coming in the door.

"You're Lee?" The man moved easily into the room. Lean, dark haired. Indian heritage, Natalie guessed from the tone of his skin and the angular lines of his face and nose. She reached for the paper just coming out of the printer and set it aside with the receipts.

"Natalie is too much of a mouthful, so most people just call me Lee. What can I do for you?"

"Sorry, that must have sounded a little chauvinistic. I was just expecting a guy. I guess I didn't ask questions, I just assumed.......From what I heard.....I'm afraid I've been caught a little off guard...."

"So it appears." She replied with a smile of amusement. "Let me finish up here, one quick minute and then you can have my complete and undivided attention." She folded the paper in half, tucked in the stack of receipts, slipped the whole into an envelope folder and turned to place it in a file drawer behind her. Then she turned back to find the man studying the wall map of Ghost Cave Mountain.

She went to stand near and nodding at the map, she asked, "Have you been here before?"

"Once. A long time ago. I was just a kid, really. We were visiting my grandfather and he took me up on the mountain. But I grew up with stories of it."

"I did, too." Her voice was soft, reflective.

He glanced at her, and then turned his attention back to the map. "You have relief maps? I came to spend some time up there. I was kinda hoping Lee McDougal could give me some pointers, some guidance about the area."

"You can get the maps at the visitor center and brochures that show all the camping areas, hiking trails and boat ramps as well as information on the park, the mountain, its history and places of interest in the area. What did you need me for?"

"Well......I was kinda hoping.....but I was expecting a man."

Natalie laughed. "I'm sorry to disappoint you, but what could Lee the man do that Lee the woman can't?"

"I'm not sure I am disappointed." He mused as he looked her over more closely, "but I just can't put forward the offer I had planned."

"You're beating around the bush! You came looking for me. Maybe I can't help you, but I may know someone who can."

"Look, I heard your boss telling you that you could leave early. Could we go somewhere cooler so that I can talk to you about this? I...I know this sounds strange and all, but now my plans will have to change and I need to explain more fully what I need in order for you to help me. Does that make sense? Just tell me where I can meet you….. somewhere cooler than this. I saw a small café just down the road, next to the service station. Can I meet you there? In….say…a half hour? Will that give you time to finish up here? That gives me time to get the maps, brochures, guides and camping permits."

"Make it an hour. You'll need that time just to wade through the paperwork and I can finish up here and close up proper."

An hour later, Natalie slid into a booth opposite the man from the office. Two glasses of ice water sat on the table in front of him. He closed a park brochure as she slid in and set it aside.

"I took the liberty of ordering iced tea. I hope you don't mind."

"Not at all. Sounds good actually."

"Thanks for meeting me like this. I really appreciate it. By the way, my name is Trace Horn. I apologize again for earlier….about your name and all. See, my cousin, Will Bartleson grew up here, went to school here and a couple years ago my Grampa passed away and we talked about this place….the mountain more precisely….Will's older than you, so you probably never met him - he left before he graduated - right after his Mom died. But our family use to live here - a long time ago – when my Grampa was young. And his family lived here, too…..not right here, but in this area. Will talked about a teacher he had in school…said he collected stories about the mountain and knew it well. At the hotel this morning, I asked the girl at the desk if she knew anyone who knew the mountain. She said there was no person knew it better than Lee McDougal and I just assumed that Lee was the teacher Will had talked about. When she told me that I could find Lee at the Park Office, I didn't ask any other questions except 'where could I find Lee McDougal'."

The iced tea arrived and the water glasses were refilled. As she listened, Natalie watched the man across the table from her. She found him attractive, a bit rough maybe from being outdoors so much. She wondered what he did, but almost as if he had read her mind, he continued.

"I was too busy playing at life to come do this sooner. But last year I saw Will again when I went to work on his uncle's ranch. We talked about doing this together this summer, but he died in a car wreck last winter. So I decided to see if his old teacher would take me up on the mountain, show me around, share his stories with me and I could share mine with him. But I can't ask a woman to go traipsing around in the wilds with a stranger for a week or so."

"How long are you planning on staying?" She asked.

"That depended on the mountain. Now I don't know. I guess I need to find the teacher Will talked about. Do you know who he is? Where I could find him? You said you were raised on stories. Would you share them with me?"

"What's your interest in the mountain?" She returned.

He set his glass down slowly, looking into the amber liquid before raising his eyes to meet hers. "My family lived in the shadow of the mountain. They lived on it, at its base, around it. It provided homes, food and life. They lived here, they died here and some are still on the mountain. I guess you could say that I came to pay homage to them...to get a sense of belonging that I lost in the city...to find my roots...to find me. Maybe I can make some sense out of who I am before I can move on to do more with my life... be who I really am... without fear and doubt."

"You don't strike me as a man with fears."

"Everyone has fears. Most just don't like to admit it or face them. My Grampa use to tell me that. He said that you don't live life to its fullest potential until you have faced your fears and come to grips with them, whether you conquer them or not. Most people, for instance, fear death. But you can't conquer death – it wins every time...with everyone...you can't escape it. So you admit your fear, acknowledge it to yourself, then set it aside and give the utmost energy to living, challenge life to give its best to you and live like you know it's right there. Honor the people you know, honor the job you do, honor your home, your land. You will find good all around you, you will be rewarded for excellence and dedication, your home will always be happy and so will you. His words...not mine...he lived them and he tried to teach those around him the same."

"I think I like your Grandfather. Did you check out of the hotel already?"

"No, I thought I'd get an idea of where to go next, what steps to take, maybe take a day or two to figure out a plan for accomplishing my mission."

"Good. Then finish your tea and follow me. We'll start out at the library…we still have a couple of hours before it closes. There are some small cool private study rooms there. We can talk without being interrupted. We can lay some maps out and I can go over some places that I know with you. Sound good to you?"

"More than good. You lead, I'll follow." He finished his tea, set the glass aside, slid out of the booth and stopped at the counter to pay before following her out.

Lee watched as he stepped into a deep blue, newer model 4x4 pickup with Wyoming plates. Out of habit, she made a mental note of the plate to jot down later. She'd give it to Sheriff Greer to see if he'd do a quick check on it for her. From the little amount of time she had spent with him, she didn't think he was hiding anything, nor did he come across as the type of fellow one would have to be wary and cautious of.

As a matter of fact, she mused, for the first time since leaving Missoula, a man had caught her interest. She had dated Dan Abbot for nearly three months before finding out that he was married. Before that it had been Bill Fordinger in college. Captain of the senior basketball team, vice president of the chess club and on path to be an architectural engineer. They had laughed a lot, had a lot of fun, but he tolerated her outdoor adventures more than got involved in them. Fishing, he could handle, but mountain hiking was just too much like work for Bill. When he graduated two years ahead of her, there hadn't been much left to keep in touch for. He had been offered a job in Boise and the last time she had seen him was after the last graduation party, when he had taken her back to the dorm. He had held her at arm's length and said, "Well, kid, it's been fun. Work hard, stay out of trouble and maybe our paths will across again someday. Right now, you got two more years here and a lot more people to meet without hangin on to someone too far to hold hands with."

Trace Horn. Lean and muscular without looking as if he spent time working out in the gym. Dark hair and deep gray eyes that had seemed to soften when he looked into her own faded jade green eyes. Before she stepped out of the truck in the library parking lot, she glanced into the rear view mirror. No lipstick, a light touch of make-up to bring out the color of her eyes. Shoulder length red hair that was sun bleached to strawberry blond with soft natural curls. "Not bad." She thought as she ran her fingers through it to soften it even more.

Trace met her at the door and followed her inside. She led him to one of three small study rooms just past a long narrow conference room with a huge plate glass window that gave a view of the entire library floor. She closed the door behind him as he laid a roll of maps on the table.

"First, let's talk about the stories." She invited as she dropped into a wide soft chair and looked up in invitation.

He pulled a matching chair closer to hers, sat and stretched his legs out. For a moment, he studied her in silence, his eyes holding hers as if reading her.

"My stories go back generations. When the first people came to this mountain, they found life here. Is that how far back you want to start the stories? My grandfather lived near here; he spent a lot of time on the mountain as he grew up. It was his back yard, his school room.

For the native people who came here, the mountain was known as the Guardian. Not so much for its height, but because it was itself a maze of streams, waterfalls, valleys, glens, ridges, saddlebacks and caves and because the foothills at its base created the same. It provided many different terrains for a large group of people to disappear in and remain hidden and safe for some time."

Natalie sat up with interest. Not unnoticed by Trace. He cocked his head to one side and lifted an eyebrow.

"Didn't know about the caves? Was the teacher someone you knew? Didn't he tell you?"

"The teacher was my father." Natalie replied softly. "He loved the mountain and the stories. He researched the history, but I'm afraid he was missing some of the early stuff from your story. He...we...explored the mountain. I don't recall he ever mentioned caves or knew about any either. I thought it was called Ghost Cave because of old mining accidents when shafts caved in and left miners buried."

"Oh, no! Ghosts on the mountain are probably as old as the mountain itself." His eyes twinkled as he eyed her. "Don't you think that almost every mountain on earth has a ghost story as old as time? Some stories pass down through the people and some die for lack of interest and audience. I don't suppose too many here abouts or even in the early days cared much about ghosts on this mountain or any other because it had no connection to them."

"Then how did you learn the stories?"

"My grandfather. Remember this was where he spent a lot of time growing up. His grandparents told him as theirs had done many times. And there is more than one ghost story for Ghost Cave Mountain."

"Why aren't they part of the local legends? Lord knows local lore covers days back to fur trapping, gold mining and Indian wars."

"Some of the earliest people to live here told stories to protect their home when they found that fear and superstition kept people away. Some of the stories were probably enlarged upon just for that purpose. My grandfather talked about caves on the mountain, but he never took us there. He may never have been to them, although he talked as if he had, or he may have decided that their whereabouts was best left unknown. He talked about caves used for burial and some used by old Indian Shamans. I'm surprised they didn't find caves during logging operations."

"Ghost Cave was never really cleared like some mountains. They only did some sections – ones that were easy to get to and get the logs out. There's a lot of old virgin timber on that mountain, despite fires over the years. Steep ravines and almost unsurpassable terrain has kept a good amount of the mountain pristine and untouched. So then does Ghost Cave have to do with old burials?"

"It was called the Guardian for a long time and then after the caves were found, some said ghosts stayed on the mountain and that they lived in the caves. Some said that the Shamans made the ghosts or called them to protect the caves of the ancestors and the sacred caves they used themselves. And for all anyone really knows, there may not be any caves, they may have been made up as convenient places for ghosts to live and hide until the Shamans needed them.

Now it's your turn, Lee. Is it OK if I call you Lee? Tell me about the mountain you know. Tell me about your father. Can I meet him?"

She got up, walked to the table and unrolled a set of maps she had brought in from her own truck.

"My stories aren't nearly as old as yours. I learned them all from my father. He went up on the mountain two years ago and never came back. But these are maps that my father and I made of sites we explored on the mountain. Here, I'll show them to you. I don't know if you'll find what you're looking for here. I don't know if any of these locations has or had any significance for your grandfather or any of your family. A good number of them are within easy hiking distance if you know which road to use to get close. Some are open to the public very near some of the hiking trails. Some are way off the trail and you really need to know how to read the map or you will get lost."

"What kind of sites?" He asked as he stepped close to look over her shoulder.

"There are a couple of old mining towns – if you can call them that. They were probably never more than tent cities with a few clapboard buildings or combined tarp and log with a few small logs houses and maybe even some tar paper shacks. The most substantial buildings remaining were probably mining offices and a hotel or saloon/hotel combination and they are falling down. Old records really don't tell much about them. One record mentions a place called Gold Rush. Several gold shipments were made from the assay office there. Population seemed to be seasonal. It may be the site highest on the mountain – there are two old shafts – one was sealed by a cave in during working days and the other was blown during logging days. There are the remains of at least a half dozen buildings, one with rusty cables and an ore car. The other is about five miles on the back side of the mountain – off the lower falls road. We know that was called Oreton. Both silver and gold. A dozen buildings remain there; a couple in fairly good shape, the rest pretty dilapidated. There was even a school there and a church that may have had a small cemetery, but only broken pieces of wood litter the back of the church and a couple of large stones that may have served as headstones. Then there are more than a half dozen sites with partial shafts or short shafts that were probably worked off and on.

But I'm guessing that what holds the most interest for you is the old fort at Low's Crossing or one of the rendezvous sites, either at the lower falls or at the convergence of Scatter Creek and Howler Creek."

As she spoke about each site she touched the map to pinpoint the location. He leaned over the map to see the notes and markings and to study the details that had been added for personal use.

She breathed in his clean male scent and was surprised at the effect on her. She resisted the impulse to reach out and touch his arm, to guide his hand to pinpoint locations. Her breath caught as he turned to look up at her as he pointed to a mark on the map.

"What's this?"

"We couldn't ever come to a real clear decision of what that was. Dad found a huge rock in the river near there that seems to have some manmade marks on it. Could have been made by fur trappers, loggers, hikers, could have marked an old ferry crossing. Just a couple of lines, but they don't look like they were made by any natural means. And then Dad found a couple of arrow heads and then I found two or three. Maybe something happened there, maybe not. But we marked it simply because we found artifacts there."

"And this?" His finger touched another spot.

"Birch trees with bark peeled. A good number of them. Maybe the bark was used to make a canoe? Several hundred yards west and up the slope is a small clearing where there are two large flat rocks, scorched. And three circles of rocks. An old campsite? There were more broken arrowheads there and a small cache of river clam shells – some had holes drilled in them."

"I think I'd like to see both of these. Are they easy to find? Or am I going to have to find a guide?"

"I'll mark one of your maps tonight and get it back to you tomorrow. Which hotel are you at?" She rolled her maps, secured them with a narrow band and reached for his.

"I'm at the Lodestar. I've taken up most of your afternoon so can I buy you dinner?" He held the door for her and followed her out. On the top step, she turned to look up at him.

"Thanks, but I have plans for the evening." She didn't, but she didn't want him to think that she was an easy pick up with no life in a small town. "I'll call you early. Have a good evening." With that she dashed down the steps, hurried back to her truck, tossed in the maps and turned the key.

Trace watched her leave, then walked slowly back to his own truck. 'Interesting girl.' He thought as he pulled back out on the street. He decided to drive around town and get his bearings.

There wasn't much to the town. A few banks, hardware store, two lumber stores, the ever present strip malls springing up in small towns, a couple of good sized grocery stores, several dry cleaners, a row of bars, clothing store, gift shops, used book store, thrift shop, churches, drug store, movie rentals, repair shops, appliance center, furniture store, fast food places and a handful of hotels. He passed two trailer parks on the way back to the motel on the edge of town and at the last traffic light recognized Lee's truck making a left turn into the grocery store across the street.

The Lodestar was tucked back behind a thin row of towering Douglas Fir. A single yellow star winked above the entrance gate that arched over the driveway. He drove past the office and continued down to park in front of #12 at the end.

He had left the air conditioning on low, so the room was comfortably cool. The bed was made, fresh towels hung and his bag still open on the bag stand. He washed up and went to have dinner in the small alcove off the front lobby.

While he waited for salad and chicken fried steak, he sipped a cold beer. As he looked around the room with its few customers, he realized that he hadn't thought of Barbara since he got up that morning. There had been few days in the past four years that she hadn't been the first thought of the day. She was one of the reasons he was here now. She had called him New Year's Day from the airport and told him that she couldn't live a lie anymore. She was on her way to Dallas with a friend and didn't plan on coming back. She couldn't identify with him she had said among other things. He had spent months sorting through her words, agonizing over the implications and trying to put his life back together. He and Will had talked off and on about Ghost Cave Mountain and the possibility of a summer visit. Then one Friday night in February, Will didn't come home after taking his pay check to town. The Sheriff came as daylight broke. Fresh snow...icy road...sharp curve...Will wouldn't be coming home. Barbara's words haunted him through the following weeks. Finally three weeks ago, he gave notice, packed his bags and hit the road. He hadn't really had a plan until last week when he saw the mountain on a post card in a road side truck stop. Maybe he could find the answers on the mountain. Maybe he could find himself, though he didn't understand why or how.

The mountain wasn't even home for him. Had been to his father, but he had met Lillian Shay in Santa Barbara when he was stationed there in the military. Then he went to Viet Nam and never came back. Lillian married another soldier when Trace was six and Trace's life turned upside down. He listened in fearful silence to the accusations when Alan got drunk. He felt the anger and resentment that grew worse after his baby sister Angela was born. Finally Lillian had called his Aunt Rose and he had gone to live with her and Uncle Charles in north western Wyoming. And he didn't see his mother again for 13 years. He went to visit her after going through flight school and he'd met his half-sister Angela and two step brothers, Todd and little Alan. Blond, blue eyed youngsters who had watched him with a hint of fear and quailed at his stepfather's cold harsh remarks. He never went back.

His father had been a late baby, so by the time Trace went to live with his Aunt Rose, her two sons were already teenagers. His grandmother had passed and health problems forced his grandfather to come live with them. His grandfather had been the one ray of light in his life, making his father come alive in stories and when he found he had an avid listener he drew into his own growing years as well. Trace felt as if he had never really belonged anywhere in his life. He had no sense of family, no real ties to anyone anymore. He had known his father through his grandfather, and maybe the mountain would let him gain some insight into the world his grandfather had opened up to him...a world most wanted to close up. Now more than ever, he needed and wanted the wisdom and comfort his grandfather had given so freely and the mountain seemed the best place to find it.

Karen J. Simon

# CHAPTER 3

Natalie was on her second cup of coffee by the time Trace met her in the Lodestar café.

"You gotta get up early if you're goin up on the mountain." She quipped cheerily as she slid a roll of maps across the table. "This time, I took the liberty of ordering for you. Coffee, bacon, eggs and a side order of toast. You can follow me up to the trailhead and I'll leave you there. There's a place to park your truck. It will be safe; not many people up there, but everyone looks out for everyone else. I packed a picnic lunch for you and several bottles of cold water. Cold roast beef on rye with white cheese, a bag of homemade trail mix and beef jerky, two Hersey bars and a Snickers. If you're not back at the trailhead by six, I'll call in the scouts. That gives you plenty of time to check out the rock at the river ford and one of the rendez sites down river about a mile. Are you ready to do this?"

"Wow! I'm a little overwhelmed by all of this. Coffee is good, and I even have time for bacon and eggs after all? And you didn't really have to fix my lunch, even though it does sound great."

"I know. You're probably thinking I'm a pushy, busy body woman taking control. Maybe…a bit. But

I want you to use the maps to find easy spots, get a feel for the land, the mountain. And believe me, if you plan on mountain hiking in the heat, the last thing you want is a heavy meal to start out and besides that you don't have time if you want to get all this in one day. If we get going shortly, you should be at the ford by a little after noon. You can eat there and take some time to wander and look around casually on your way down river. By the time you get there, you'll have a better idea of time, speed and distance for getting back. While you're out there, I'll map out some possible spots for tomorrow and maybe by Monday you'll be ready to go in for a couple of days. Do you have a fishing license? Fishing gear?"

"I didn't plan on fishing. Look, you don't have to spend your whole weekend babysitting me. I've been on my own before."

"I've no doubts. But if you plan on being out there for a few days, fishing gear helps in case you need extra food – mountain water fish are pretty good grilled on a hot rock, or over an open fire, you know."

"OK, I'll admit that my mountain experience is a little lacking. But I did grow up at the foot of the mountains in western Wyoming. I have taken hunter safety courses and I did pass wilderness survival course in the military."

"Unfortunately, you managed to dump yourself on my desk, and the park and the mountain are part of my job responsibilities. I know there a lot of people go in and hike that have never been here or done this before, but they stick to the trails. All mountains were not created equal and you have no intention of staying anywhere near the trails. Besides, I have more food in the fridge at home than I can get rid of in this heat. Enjoy it while I feel hospitable. Here's your toast."

It promised to be a beautiful day with clear blue skies. On the mountain, it would be cool along the shaded paths and even the open spaces would be cooler than the valley floor. She parked her truck and he parked next to hers. Before opening her door she reached for the two bags on the front seat, one containing the lunch she had prepared and one the extra water. Trace dropped the tailgate of his pick-up, set his backpack up and set the rolled maps alongside of it. Natalie placed the two bags beside them and Trace unzipped the main compartment to set in the lunch and water bottles. He unrolled the maps, laid them out and folded them neatly before placing them into a front pocket of the bag. He lifted the bag, slung it over his shoulders and readjusted the straps, then followed Natalie to the trailhead.

"I'd really like to go along, but duty calls." She sighed. "Just follow the trail in for about a mile, when it turns downhill you'll see a game trail to the left. Take the game trail and follow it up til you get to the burn area. You'll be looking up toward a rock face. At the base of that rock face is an exposed area of bedrock. A good place to rest in the shade, lay out your maps, look over the land, get your bearings and rest before going on. Have fun, enjoy your day and I'll see you back here later this evening."

Trace adjusted his hat, looked up the trail. "The company would be great. But I think I am looking forward to some solitude. Something in the air, maybe. Thanks. I'll see you back here. Don't work too hard."

Natalie watched as he set out upon the trail, then turned back to her pick-up. By ten, she was back in town and parking at the Sheriff's Office.

"Well, if this is who owns the truck and all ID is current and correct, he comes up clean." Greer said as she entered his office. "Here, I poured you coffee when I saw you pull up. How's your Mother?"

"Enjoying family, friends and old home town. The house is quiet without her, though. But she really needed to get away. I should have insisted she do this a year ago, I guess I just wasn't ready to lose her, too. I checked at the library and a Will Bartleson did go to school here. No school photos, no information."

"Yeah, I checked on him, too. Family wasn't the best in town, Lee. South of town - Squatters Ridge...itinerant farm people, Indians. Bartleson's not Indian, though. Couldn't find that he ever got into trouble. His mother died in a car wreck. His father disappeared shortly afterwards. Probably same time he did. Thing is, I can't find any Horns anywhere in this area. Odd name. You'd think if the family had been here a long time, some would still be here. Don't see the name listed anywhere – schools, birth, deaths, land. But that doesn't mean anything with computers these days. Too many variables. All I can tell you for sure is that I can't find any wants or warrants for a Trace Horn – anywhere."

Lee set down the coffee cup. "Had enough for one day. Thanks Sheriff Greer."

She headed home to lay maps out on the table and put together a workable short term schedule for seeing as many of the sites in as short a time as possible.

Karen J. Simon

# CHAPTER 4

The sun was reaching its zenith in a cloudless brilliant blue sky. In the shelter of the trees it was still cool, but as he made his way carefully across a shale slope, the sun beat without mercy upon all foolish enough to leave the shade. He had taken off his shirt and stuffed it into his backpack not long after leaving the trees and rubbed a liberal amount of lotion onto his exposed skin. Another two hundred yards and he stepped onto a large outcropping of rock that stretched another one hundred or so yards. He glanced down to his left and somewhere below heard the sound of rushing water. This must be the small narrow gorge just above the meadow clearing. He picked his way among some scattered boulders and suddenly found himself facing a deep six foot chasm. He turned and worked his way uphill, again skirting around and climbing over boulders and more solid rock outcroppings until the chasm narrowed enough to get across. Across a barren section of rock, he found that he stood on a rocky ridge. He squatted down to look both directions hoping to find an easy way down. Finding none, he stood and walked another distance before repeating the observation. Finally he found a gentle slope that once again offered a terrain of scattered boulders to pick through. But across these was an old burn area with gray stumps showing above tall wavering grasses. A thin line of trees beyond and at last he broke into the small meadow. He found the stones and paused a moment to study them. Any forest fire could have created the burn damage, but when he dug at the base of one, he found the soil a mixture of ash. Too much for one or two forest fires. He kept digging and discovered what Lee and her father had upon closer inspection. The somewhat flat stone sat above an old fire pit. His flashlight reflected off metal and he reached in to pull out a can and dumped the contents on the surface of the stone. He picked up each one, ran his fingers along the ragged edge of an obsidian arrowhead, wondering where it had come from, who had made it. One was flatter and wider at the base than the others, almost transparent at its tip. He slipped that one into his pocket, scooped the remainder of the items into the can and set it just under the lip of the stone. Picking up the lunch bag, he headed for the sound of running water, noting the scarred birch trees as he passed through the small grove. The creek was wide, clear and shallow, its waters barely contained in the bed of gravel it flowed over.

Trace squatted, dipped his hands into the cold flow and lifted handfuls to splash over his face and hair. It was cooler here by the creek and in the shadow of the birch trees. Just up creek, a fallen tree arched across the water, the perfect picnic bench. As he ate his sandwich, he surveyed his surroundings, lost in a myriad of thoughts. On his own, he wouldn't have paid attention to the two flat rocks and the stripped birch bark would not have caught his attention. Without Lee, this would have just been a walk in the wilderness. He chuckled to think of the irritation he had felt this morning when she laid out the day for him. But as he sat in the silence, a blanket of peace settled around him and he was grateful for her effort. He took the arrowhead out of his pocket and turned it over and around between his fingers. The workmanship was beautiful and precise. Primitive, but as he admired the skill of the knapper, he felt a new admiration and respect for these unknown people. A twig snapped breaking the silence and he looked up quickly almost expecting to see a buckskin clad figure emerge from the trees.

"Well," He mused softly, "buckskin, but not human. Hi little fella. Didn't expect company? Don't mind me, I just came to watch and go." His voice low enough not to startle the fawn that trembled at the edge of trees. For some time, they eyed each other in silence, then the fawn stepped tentatively forward to drop his velvet nose into the water. With one more glance in Trace's direction, the fawn suddenly leapt forward, splashed across the creek and sprinted into the woods on the far side.

Trace brushed crumbs off his lap, opened one of the water bottles and took a long swallow before slipping off his perch. He walked through the grove of birch, fingering the scars on those stripped of bands of bark. Then on impulse, he pulled the arrowhead from his pocket and studying the cut, he touched the edge of the tool to the bark and applied a small amount of pressure. He was surprised at how easily the sharp edge cut through the paper like bark.

He cut a line downward about six inches, then took the curling edge of bark and pulled gently. The bark pulled away with little effort and soon he held the piece rolled like an ancient scroll. He leaned against the tree and closed his eyes. A canoe? Out of this insubstantial material? Surely once it was dry it would be brittle and fragile. What else had these people used birch bark for? Clothes? Baskets? Cradles? And how had they held the pieces together? Living off the land suddenly didn't seem to be as easy and simple as some people liked to think - at least in the absence of a super mall.

He almost left the curled up piece of bark in the fire pit, but at the last moment, pushed it into the backpack. He held the arrowhead in the palm of his hand, turned it once more in his fingers and placed it gently into the can, replaced the can in the pit and scooped the soil ash mixture back into the hole, pulled some grasses to push into the mixture and with a quick look around went in search of the ford.

Finding the ford was easier. He just followed the creek a short distance until its waters joined the rushing water of the river. And there were the rocks in the center of the river. He dropped his pack and waded in. The cold water made his breath catch, but he continued on. At the rocks, the water was about chest deep and rushing at a good clip as it picked up speed going downhill. His foot slipped on a loose rock and he reached out to wrap an arm around the nearest rock, scraping his ribs along a jagged edge. He cursed softly under his breath and began working his way carefully around the rock, only to find that on the uphill side, the depth had changed to about waist deep. He took a moment to lean against the rock, and survey the damage to his burning ribs. From front to back, the lower part of his right rib area was scraped raw. A thin line of blood marked the two deepest gashes. Not serious enough to need stitches nor to divert attention long from the rocks against which he braced himself. Nothing about the nearer one seemed out of place, so he moved slowly to the right and felt his way toward the most forward rock. The water depth increased until he sucked in his breath as it washed the raw skin over his ribs. But he had reached the forward rock. It stood like a sentinel slightly to the right and forward of the first with barely a hands breadth separating them. Several inches above the water line two lines had been scored into the rock all round its circumference. A finger width apart, they were as deep as they were thick. He studied them for a moment, then turned to scan the shoreline on either side. Ropes that marked rock like this should also have scarred trees. But had rope made the impressions? It was between the two rocks that he found the markings on the first. Four horizontal zig zag lines about four or five inches long below the level of the lines on the sentinel rock, but still above the water line. A quarter of the way around the other side, were three more lines in the same manner. As he looked closer he found two more almost at the rear of the rock. He had missed them because of his stumble and he would have missed them altogether if he had not known they were there.

He was more cautious returning to shore, where he searched the trees for some tell-tale mark that would indicate the rocks may have been part of a ferry system. He found nothing and no sign that trees had fallen or been removed.

Little time remained to make it to the rendezvous site, so Trace picked up his pace and hurried down river. There wasn't much to see when he arrived at the large low meadow at the bend in the river. It was a perfect spot for a large encampment, with a sweeping view of the river in both directions and a wide rock strewn beach on both sides of the river. A large number of tree stumps and portions of old logs littered the open area. He could almost imagine canoes pulled onto the shore, some piled high with cured furs and stacks of trade goods laid out on shore and ready for barter while men of both races wandered through the mayhem. Men and horses would have laid the tall meadow grasses down to carpet the ground. At night, with the moon low in the sky, camp fires would have winked up and down the river, the air heavy with wood smoke and the aroma of roasted meat. Laughter, voices and the soft nickering of a horse would have broken the silence of the mountain.

No place he had ever been had affected him like the places he had visited today. None had given him such a feeling of connection to the world about him. For the first time in his life he caught an insight to the depth of peace inside of his grandfather. He understood the lack of harsh judgment and anger. It didn't exist out here. There was only silence, deep peace, full acceptance, the gentle passing of time.

The sun was settling lower in the sky, shadows lengthening in the clearings, and darkness growing in the woods. As he climbed uphill, Trace became more and more aware of the ache on his right side. The strap of the backpack sat on the upper part and rubbed even after he put his shirt back on to lessen the contact. His step slowed in hopes of lessening the rubbing, but by the time he stepped onto the path back to the truck, he could feel the trickle of blood down his side. He knew he was late and hoped that Lee hadn't called out the troops.

Karen J. Simon

# CHAPTER 5

It was nearly seven when Lee pulled up alongside of Trace's truck and realized that he was nowhere around. He should be waiting for her, but instead his truck sat deserted and alone at the trailhead – deserted and alone – just like her father's had. It didn't matter that Trace was no stranger to the out of doors, had taken hunter safety and passed wilderness survival. Her father had done all of that and more. Her father had known this mountain like he knew his own back yard and still something had happened. Trace thought he could handle himself out here, so had her father. He was a grown man, he could handle anything. But dad blast it! It was her mountain! And he had come to her looking for help about finding places of interest! And she had sent him into the same areas she and her father had been many times. Areas that could well have taken her father's life. She knew that if anything happened to Trace, she would feel responsible. Thoughts tumbled and jumbled as the minutes passed and her agitation and anxiety increased. Half an hour later, she headed down the trail and met him just coming around the first bend.

"Sorry, I'm late." He apologized sheepishly. "Are the scouts on the way in?"

"No, I was late myself. But since you're late, follow me home and we'll go over the maps I've marked for you. We can lay them out on the table there. How was it? Did you get lost?"

He winced as he lifted the backpack free and pulled open the truck door with his right hand, hoping she wouldn't notice. She tipped her head to one side and looked up at him.

"Tired? You shouldn't be sore, but you may be tomorrow if you overdid the uphill."

"I'm fine," He grinned at her, tugged off his hat and wiped sweat from his face with his free hand. "and ready any time you are."

He waited for her to turn her back and walk to her truck before he stepped into his own, catching his breath as he did.

Lee took her time going down the mountain, but every bump jarred Trace's now fully aching ribs and he began to wonder if he had done more than just scrape them. He would have to do a quick bow out once they got to her place. After the fuss he'd made about being able to hold his own out there, he didn't want her to see that he goofed on his first day out.

It was past dark when they pulled up in front of Lee's place. The back door was open and light flooded the steps as Trace came up them. He pushed open the screen and stepped into the kitchen. Lee placed a steaming cup of hot coffee on the table and then moved to the stove.

"Hungry?" She asked as she opened the refrigerator door and turned back with a platter of ham.

"Starved."

"Well, I can't fix that. Ham and warm rice with green peas and onions will have to do. There's a half bath on the left down the hall. Clean wash cloth and towels. Help yourself while I finish up here."

A sink full of warm water and soap took the dust from the hiking. He bent gingerly over the sink and ran soapy water over his hair, then tugged off his shirt and dabbed at the raw red patch of skin over his rib cage, wincing as the rough material of the cloth touched tender skin. For a moment he leaned against the wall, breathing deeply, fighting the urge to moan his hurt. The bleeding had stopped, but his shirt had a bit of stain on it. When he lifted his arms to put his shirt back on, he bumped his elbow on the corner of the wall cabinet that earned him a double "Ouch!" when he pulled back hard enough to press against the sore ribs.

Lee shouted from the kitchen, "You OK in there?"

"Sorry. Banged the wall cabinet with an elbow. Didn't chip any paint though."

"Good thing, paintings' not on my list this summer. Feel better? Go ahead and sit down. Coffee's getting cold and the rice is almost ready. Not fancy hotel food, but it'll fill the gaps."

"Smells good." He studied her over the rim of his coffee cup as he leaned back against a counter. Her back was turned and his eyes slid over the contours of her body. Blue jeans that fit every curve, powder blue t-shirt. Her reddish blond hair fell in soft waves to her shoulders. He hadn't seen any evidence of a man in residence, so she must live alone, yet he didn't have the feeling that she did. She moved with an easy grace that made him want to reach out and touch her, to feel the tenderness beneath the air of confidence, but he didn't want to scare her. He didn't want to reach for something he couldn't have.

As if she read his thoughts, she turned with a bowl of steaming rice, caught his look and paused. There was a hint of tremor in her voice when she spoke. "Sit. You make me nervous standing around watching."

"Didn't mean to make you nervous. You're kinda easy on the eyes. It's a pleasure to watch someone move with ease and grace around a kitchen. Almost gives a feeling of being at home."

"Flattery isn't on the menu. Let me warm your coffee and over eating you can tell me how your day went. What did you see? What did you think?"

"I saw everything on the list." He said as he pulled a chair away from the table and sat down, "Fascinating. I would have missed so much if you hadn't told me it was there. How did you find the places?"

"I didn't. My Dad did." She replied as she set down fresh cups of coffee for both of them and slipped onto a chair opposite him. "He was a teacher…history…and he loved the legends and lore of this place…He talked to anyone and everyone who would share, he went out looking for the history to make it alive for the stories he wrote and the classes he taught. Ancient cultures fascinated him, he wanted to learn everything there was to know about them – who they were, where they came from, where they lived, how they lived – and died. He'd spend hours in one spot, just sitting and looking, wondering what appeal the spot might have. Anything and everything caught his eye and he studied it carefully to see if it was natural or had some helping hand in being where and how it was. He did it for years and as I grew up and tagged along, he shared it with me. Everything he found, he left there….cached it somewhere close to something…stuffed in old tin cans, leather pouches, whatever he carried along easily. It only has value on that site, so it just never seemed right to remove it. Away it had no significance, there it was part of whatever went on there."

"I found the can at the flat rocks, beautiful craftsmanship on the arrowheads. I figured that you and your Dad did that…left the stuff there that is."

"You did? You found it?" There was excitement in her voice. "You actually found the can? I can't believe it! I didn't expect you to….."

"I was being nosey…Trying to figure out if the stones had been damaged by continued exposure to forest fires."

They ate in silence and she studied him when she thought he wasn't looking. His hair was damp from washing and he smelled of soap. Clean…masculine.

Suddenly she dropped her fork and looked at him. "Why did you really come here?" She had not meant to be demanding, but there was something about him that made her cautious, made her want to really know the truth he seemed to be skirting.

That softened her voice, gave it a gentle caring quality that touched Trace deeply. He pushed his plate away as he pushed his chair back to stand quickly. "I really ought to be going." He said roughly. But the swift movements made him suck his breath in hard. He moved toward the door as she got up and moved after him. She placed her hand on his arm as he stopped to open the door and the movement pressed his right arm into his side and this time the soft moan escaped before he could stop it.

"Trace! What's wrong? Are you OK? I'm sorry. I didn't mean to sound as if I were probing into your personal life." She turned him toward her and put even more pressure on his ribs. He reached out to grab the door jam, trying to pull away from the pressure. Not realizing that she was applying pressure to an injury, she pushed his arm in an effort to turn him to her.

"Aaahhh!" He gasped. "Don't!" He put his hand over hers to push it way as he tried to draw his right arm away from his side. She stepped back as he pulled the door and staggered out onto the steps. He paused for moment to get his breath, then continued down and moved unsteadily to the truck. It was an effort to get in, and he sagged back against the seat, closing his eyes. He had no sooner turned the ignition when the door opened.

"Trace? Please, I don't know what I did, but I'm sorry. What happened? Are you OK?"

"I'm fine. Really. I slipped and fell today. Got a few bruises. Dumb. But I really need to go lie down and get some rest. You have been better than the best. Lunch, dinner. I owe you lots."

"We didn't get a chance to go over your maps. Why didn't you tell me that you fell?"

"It was stupid. I wasn't watching my step. I'll be OK. I've had worse!"

She closed the door and watched as he drove carefully out of the yard and down the lane.

"Trace Horn, there's something you're not telling me." She said as she cleaned up the kitchen. "Something you're running from." She finished and leaned against the counter, folding her arms. "A woman? No ring, but that doesn't mean a thing. Are you running from her or did she run from you? I got a feeling she dumped you. Pity, you don't seem a bad man. A bit egotistical, but what man isn't? You are sort of attractive…and maybe a bit sexy. Go ahead. Go home. I'll see you in the morning, maybe by then I'll have slept on it and found an answer." She pushed away from the counter, turned out the lights and headed for bed.

Karen J. Simon

## CHAPTER 6

Silence was broken by the loud clanging of the phone ringer. Trace rolled over and stopped abruptly as the room spun and pain stabbed his right side. He gasped at the effort it took to roll over. Extending his right arm to grab the phone brought him up short again; his body didn't want to move. Every muscle in his chest and side screamed at every movement. It took massive effort to cast aside covers and haul his body to a sitting position on the edge of the bed. He wanted to tuck his arm into his ribs, but the skin was so tender, touching it sent searing lances of pain along every nerve. The phone rang again and this time he reached for it with his left hand, managing as he did so to knock the phone off the night table, but holding onto the handset.

"Yeah." His voice came out rough and ragged; sounded as if he had been up all night.

"Bacon and eggs? Café? Or home cooked?" Lee chirped.

"Neither. I'm a casualty and I'm calling for a truce. I need help. I need to be left alone. I need a corner to curl up in."

Lee laughed. "Make up your mind! Should I be worried? Do I need to call a doctor? Or just an ambulance?"

"Hell! I don't know what I need! I don't need a doctor! And I sure as hell don't want an ambulance! But I am sore as all billy get out. I can't move and breathin hurts. So does talkin and sittin, so make whatever fast."

"That's a start! I'll make bacon and eggs to go. Can you get up and open the door or should I ask the front desk for a spare key?"

"I'll have to move before you get here. If the doors' locked, holler loud."

"See ya!" And the phone went dead in his hand. Stooping over to pick it up was too much trouble, so he just let the handset drop onto the carpet with the rest of the phone. Then, reaching out to brace himself on the nightstand, he attempted to stand. His ribs screamed in protest, the effort sent him sinking back moaning and wishing he was anywhere but here. Every position he attempted put pressure on some tender spot. Minutes dragged by like hours and it was an eternity before the door knob rattled.

"Trace? Open up! You OK?" When he didn't reply she hollered again. "OK. That's it! You better be decent cause I'm goin to get a key!"

He couldn't help but grin, he knew laughing would hurt. Silence. And then a key, the door knob turned slowly, the door opened a bit and her voice came in...tentative... "Trace? You decent? You OK?"

"Yeah." He moaned. He had pulled the sheet up during the silence. The door opened wider.

"My God! You look like the livin dead! Are you sure you're OK? You don't want me to call the doctor? Where are you hurt? What's wrong?"

He grinned again. "Slow down!" He gasped. "Can you help me get up?"

"What do you want me to do? But first, where are you hurt? What happened?"

"I slipped and fell." He rasped. "Against the rock in the river. Got my ribs. Don't think they're broke, just bad bruised. Skin's all tore up."

"Roll over and let me see." She commanded.

He rolled slightly onto his left hip, trying to hold his right arm up enough not to touch raw skin.

"My God! Trace! Why didn't you say something? You're bruised all the way from armpit to hip and half way around your back on the ribs. You may not need an ambulance, but you're definitely going to be more comfortable with some pain killers and ointment. Whether you like it or not, we're going to have to get you to the ER."

"First you gotta get me up off this bed!" He growled. "And I'm not gonna be able to hold the sheet, so look the other way."

She laughed.

And he growled again. "And don't laugh! And don't make me laugh cause it hurts!"

She sobered as he tucked his left arm under himself and then she sat down softly and provided support for him to begin lifting his body to a sitting position, swinging his legs slowly and agonizingly back over the edge of the bed. She slid her body against his, acutely aware of the warmth of his naked skin and male scent. As his body moved, she reached across to keep the sheet over his lap.

Sitting on the edge of the bed, he turned, his face almost touching hers. Close up she was prettier than ever and he knew she was aware of his warmth, his nakedness. He could see it in her eyes. And…a softness…he suddenly wanted to touch as he had wanted to last night. He grinned. "What a way to get to know a guy, huh? The easy part's over, it's the next part's got me a mite worried. By the way, did you know you got pretty green eyes?"

"There goes the flattery again. Your eggs and bacon are getting cold so let's get this over with! What do you want me to do to make this easier?"

"Wish I knew the answer to that!" He gasped. "Stand in front of me. Let me lean forward into you to get balance, then move to my left and brace up. You'll have to take a firm hold on my upper arm…the higher, the better. The sheet will have to go. I can't hold it with my right cause I'm going to be reaching for you. And I won't be able to hold it with my left."

She stood and moved as he had directed her to. He took a deep shuttering breath and leaned forward. She moved quickly to his left and took his arm as he pushed up from the bed. The maneuver brought a softly strangled "Aahh" from him, but he was standing. She moved to his right, yanked the sheet off the bed and held it up in front of him. He took small halting steps toward the bathroom. At the door, she stepped back and he took hold of the door frame.

"I'll step out to the truck. Holler when you're ready." She backed quickly out and went to move the truck to a closer parking spot, then went to stand just outside the door until he called out to her. He was standing by the bed holding a towel in front of his body.

"In my bag." He told her. "A pair of jeans. Do you think you can help me?"

A black duffle type bag was open on the suitcase rack. She pulled the top a bit more. Socks…on top of jeans and shirts were the first thing she saw. She picked up a pair of neatly folded blue jeans and shook them out as she walked over to skirt the bed, noticing as she did that his back side was naked. The bruise on his right side actually went half way around his back up toward the shoulder blade and then angled down toward his right hip. The skin was scraped raw and scratched deeply. Three deep ragged gashes came up from under his armpit and extended nearly to the shoulder blade. He must have twisted as he fell. No wonder he was sore! Her gaze didn't miss the slender hips, the tight muscles that extended down his back to his buttocks, thighs and legs.

She came around the bed and knelt down, opening the jeans for the right leg first. She felt the pressure of his hand on the top of her head as he shifted his weight and lifted the right foot just off the floor. She slipped the jeans on quickly and settled them around the ankle before rubbing his leg to let him know she was finished. Again he shifted weight while she readied the left leg. More pressure on her head and a bit more as his weight moved all the way

Karen J. Simon

right and he lifted the left foot. She repeated the same maneuver to get his pants on and then began to tug them upwards. She stopped at the bottom of the towel and looked up to see him watching her, a smile on his lips.

"Enjoying yourself?" He asked wickedly. "Cause I am."

"Are you flirting with me?" She asked as she stood up.

"Taking advantage of a situation I have no control over, would be more apt. And I find you very attractive, which isn't very smart on my part. Now, if you can get behind me and pull up from the back, I'll take care of the front." He replied.

Her hands brushed the naked skin on the back of his legs as she took hold of the jeans and began pulling them up, her touch lingering on thighs and buttocks. As her hands moved the fabric upward, he released the towel and she couldn't help but admire the tight muscles, the shape of his upper thighs, slender hips and buttocks. Tingling sensations went through to his groin and he reacted instantly to her touch with a soft exclamation under his breath that she didn't miss though she was unaware of the cause.

"There's a pair of flip flops at the bottom of the bag. Please?" He instructed.

Ready at last, he leaned on her as he shuffled slowly to the door and out to her truck. With the passenger door open, he hesitated - assessing the new challenge of getting in and setting still for any distance. But it was a left handed lift and he turned easily into it. He reached out with his right to brace himself on the door and gritted his teeth with the effort of lifting himself up and into the seat. Lee closed the door as he turned to his left to keep his back off the seat, but twisting strained muscles and skin that were already stiff, swollen, sore and unresponsive. He tucked his left knee up on the seat and leaned his left shoulder against the back of the seat. Lee slipped behind the wheel and tossed a towel across his lap.

As she turned the truck out on to the street, she spoke softly. "I'm really sorry about this, Trace. I feel kind of responsible. I sent you out to look at those rocks. This wouldn't have happened if you'd just gone out exploring on your own."

"Don't." He replied softly. "It's not your fault. I was at the first rock when I lost my footing. I kinda threw my arm around the rock to grab it. I'll be Ok. Stiff and sore for a few days, nothing I can't handle."

"Would you consider staying at my place while you recover?" She asked tentatively.

He studied her for a moment, knowing that she was aware of his appraisal. "Are you sure about that?" His voice was nearly inaudible. "You may not want to get yourself in a situation you don't want or aren't comfortable with. I am a stranger. And I am a man and to be frank and honest, I find you very attractive."

She didn't answer immediately and when she did there was only a small bit of hesitation, uncertainty. "I am aware of all of that. I am not naïve. I mean not about your attraction," she stumbled, "but about our not knowing each other and caution.

But you're hurt and need help and even though you say I am not, I still feel some responsibility. After all, I did suggest those sites. And…honestly…I…I…and I am…I feel… a small attraction to you. But, please don't take advantage of that."

"I don't take advantage of people. I wouldn't force you into anything. I am…I was raised to treat people with respect and dignity. I've never done anything less."

"Are you married?" She asked.

"No."

"Involved?"

He hesitated just a bare moment before replying in the negative. Enough for her to feel a squeeze deep inside. A warning. He was running. She was sure of it. But why would he tell her he found her attractive? Was he a playboy? Did he expect her to play and run as well? She didn't intend to let him know how much he affected her. And she realized suddenly that she had not admitted to herself until this moment. She had looked forward to seeing him this morning. She had been affected by his nakedness, by his male scent, by his body heat, his nearness. She felt a slow burning sensation in her belly and heat flushed her face.

"Are we there, yet?" He whispered hoarsely, breaking into her reverie.

She glanced quickly over to see him grimacing against every bump. "Just two more blocks. I'm sorry."

"For what?" He cocked open an eye to look at her, wondering why she had gone so quiet. What was she thinking?

"The bumps. The hurt. The whole mess!"

At the hospital, she parked in the ER unload zone and hurried around to open the door. Trace turned slowly and nearly knocked her over when he fell more than climbed out the truck. She wrapped her arms around him to keep them both from tumbling onto the cement and he blanched as the pressure of her arms burned his skin like a hot iron. He staggered against the door and she released him instantly, realizing that in her effort to save them the fall, she had hurt him. A tear slipped from her eyes as he caught his balance and moved slowly past her, allowing her to reach in and grab the towel to place lightly over his shoulder. She stepped to his side and supported him through to the desk where she left him while she parked the truck. When she returned, he was nowhere to be seen. Questions and delays before she was allowed in the back rooms and then the room they had sent her to was empty as well. Only the towel on the bed gave evidence that he had been here. She went back out to the desk.

"Trace Horn?" She asked.

The nurse raised an eyebrow. "Who?"

"Trace Horn. The guy that was in room number three."

"Oh, him. He went to x-ray. He'll be back shortly. You his wife?"

"No. Friend." She murmured as she lowered her head and returned to the room to wait. It seemed to take forever, but then he was in a wheelchair, leaning forward, coming through the wide door. He frowned when he saw her waiting and she wondered if she had overstepped her bounds.

"No sense waiting in here." He told her. "You should go get some breakfast…some coffee…by then I'll be ready to leave."

"I'll be outside." She said quickly and left. She had been dismissed and she felt a bit hurt though she had no idea why she should. He was a stranger. Nothing to her.

It was an hour before he reappeared in the outer waiting room. Still moving slowly, but a bit more relaxed. The doctored followed, coming directly to her.

"Miss McDougal? He can go home. No broken bones. A couple cracked and they can be more painful than broken ones. Bad bruising that will last awhile. He'll be stiff and sore for about a week. I'd like him to stay quiet for a couple of days. We've given him a pretty powerful shot to dull the pain and we filled a prescription for pain pills and some ointment for the scrapes. The ointment should also help with some of the topical pain. A couple of those gashes came just short of stitches. Reduced movement will help those heal faster. A pretty nasty fall that will just take time to heal. He'll probably sleep most of today. Will you be there?"

"Yes." She said without hesitation. "I'll pull the truck up. If I could help getting him in?"

A nurse helped him get into the truck and once again he turned to pull his left knee up on the seat and tuck his left shoulder against the backrest. By the time she arrived home, he was pretty well out of it, but she managed to rouse him enough to get him out of the truck, into the house and into the back guest room. She pulled the covers aside and he dropped gently onto the bed, laying back and closing his eyes almost immediately. When he was settled, she went back into town, packed his things and turned in his room key. No sense paying for a room he wasn't using.

The house had been too quiet with her mother gone. It was still quiet, but his presence was enough to make it feel like she wasn't alone. At three, the phone rang and she rushed to answer it.

"Lee?" Her mother asked.

"Yes, Mom. How are you? I miss you. The house is so quiet!"

"I called earlier, but didn't get an answer. I was afraid that you had gone out for the weekend. I went to church this morning with Anna and her neighbor Bess Wilson. And afterwards we stopped at a flower show. The flowers are unbelievable, honey. How are you? How are things going?"

"Nothing new, Mom. Heat, heat and more heat. But thank God no fires. The AC quit working in the office so I left early on Friday. They're supposed to get it fixed tomorrow, but I'm taking the big fan in, just in case. How's everyone there?"

"Do you think I should come home? I do miss you, too, and home."

"I'm fine, Mom. Really. It's been so long since you've been there. Don't cheat yourself or anyone else of memories. Stay as long as you want to. Give some serious thought to all the things we talked about before you left. But don't hurry back on my account, Mom, I am and will continue to be just fine."

"OK, honey, then I will accept an invitation to go spend a week with my cousin Jenny. You remember her, don't you? She lives in Savanna. I think there are a couple of other cousins there, too, I don't remember, but I'll let you know. I'm putting together a journal of all the relatives just for you. It's late here, so I better go. I'll call you next weekend, OK honey?"

"I love you, Mom. Next week." Lee hung up and decided to check on Trace. Tucked over on his left side, he was sleeping peacefully. She leaned over and lightly brushed the hair from his forehead. He didn't move. Her gaze swept the length of him lying under the covers and she remembered his nakedness earlier in the day. He was attractive and he was definitely attracting her. She wondered again about the woman in his life. Why wasn't she here with him? Had they had a misunderstanding? Was he just looking for someone to soothe his hurt feelings until they patched things up? Would she be worried if he didn't call her for a few days? If she kept her thoughts going along this line, he would be less and less attractive. She wouldn't get involved with a man who had interest somewhere else. One last sweeping gaze and she turned to leave the room, closing the door softly after her.

One more time, before she went to bed, she looked in on him and found him in the same position. She turned on a small bedside lamp and watched his even breathing before feeling comfortable enough to leave him for the night.

Karen J. Simon

# CHAPTER 7

It was not the alarm that woke Lee. She tensed and listened. The house was dark and still, lit only by the yard light. She turned her head on the pillow to see the face of the clock. Four o'clock. She was certain that a sound had brought her to full wakefulness, but the house was still. Minutes ticked by and she was about to flip the covers aside when she heard another sound. A soft thump. That's what had waked her! She bounded out of bed, opened her door and listened again. Another soft thump. From the guest room! Trace! She hurried downstairs and to the bedroom door. The light was off, but the door was still closed. She turned the knob slowly and called out softly so as not to startle him.

"Trace?"

Twice more before she heard a soft moan. She pushed the door open and slipped into the room.

"Trace?"

He was sitting on the edge of the bed, rocking gently. She reached over to turn on the light, but he seemed oblivious to it. His head was tilted back as he rocked and then he raised his left foot and dropped it onto the floor with a soft 'thump'.

"Trace? It's Lee. Do you remember me? Are you alright?"

"Mmm. Lee." He nodded, then went back to rocking. "Hurts to lie down. Hurts to breath."

"The doctor gave you a prescription for pain killer. I'll go get a glass of water so you can take one. I'll be right back."

He didn't move, other than to continue the rocking and stopped only long enough to pop the pill into his mouth and wash it down with water. She made him drink all of it. Then she reached down to touch his knees and encourage him to lie back down so that she could lift his legs back onto the bed. He rolled onto his left side as she got up to pull the covers back over him. He mumbled again and she leaned closer to hear his words, her lips close to his cheek, her breath a soft caress on his skin.

"No. Can't... you'll...eave, too. Doan...leave... pleeese... doan...eave..." His words trailed off. Impulsively, she brushed her lips against his cheek and stood up.

Upstairs, she crawled back into bed and glanced at the clock. Thirty five minutes had passed since she woke up. The alarm wouldn't go off for another hour and a half. Maybe she could get in a quick nap.

The alarm woke her; dawn was just beginning to break the horizon. She slipped from her bed, made it up quickly and hurried downstairs to start coffee. While it was brewing, she went into the pantry, picked up two clean bowls from a lower shelf, dipped one into a bag of dry cat food, filled the second with fresh water from the tap and slipped out the back door and on to the shed. With her foot, she pushed the shed door open and heard the soft mewling of new kittens.

"Hi, mama." Lee whispered. "How are the little ones today? When you gonna bring them in the house and show them off, huh?" She set down the clean bowls, rubbed the tabby's soft fur and scooped up the two empty bowls. The coffee would be done by the time she went back in; the aroma filling the house, waking her up, starting her day. She poured a cup, slipped down the hall and peeked in on Trace. He was still sleeping. She tiptoed upstairs, selected clean clothes and turned the shower water on. Forty five minutes later, dressed and ready to go, she opened the door to the guest room.

"Do you always make so much noise?" Trace asked sleepily. "That smell has filled the room for an hour."

"Hasn't been made that long. I'll get you a cup in a minute. How are you feeling? Rough night?"

"I don't feel much of anything. Numb…all over. And don't feel like I could stay awake long enough to drink any coffee. Hey, were you in here last night or was I dreaming?"

"I was in here. You woke me up; scared me. I'll be right back. Don't go anywhere." And with that she was gone. And instantly back.

"Thought you left." He mumbled.

"I did. Here, sit up. Coffee, toast with honey and another pain pill."

"Scared you? How?"

75

"Aw! Neurons are firing in sequence! Will you be Ok long enough for me to go into town for a couple of hours?"

"Into town? Where am I?"

"My place. I hope you don't mind. I got your things from the hotel and checked you out. Doctor said he didn't want you alone, wouldn't look good for me to come in and out of your hotel room all hours of the night and it had only one bed if you recall. So I brought you home."

He handed her the empty plate and refused more coffee.

"You will regret that!" She set the cup and plate down and picked up a tube of ointment from the bedside table. "Cause you're gonna hate me for this next one. Lie down."

She stepped around the bed and leaned over to put a drop of ointment on his back, grimaced when he flinched at the contact. As gently as she could, she rubbed the ointment evenly into the raw skin, mindful of the scabs forming on the deeper gashes. His body tensed beneath her fingers, soft moans escaped with ragged breaths. When she finished, he relaxed, his breath coming in quick gasps.

"Sorry." She whispered, "I don't like hurting anyone, but the doctor said this would help the healing." When he said nothing, she hurried out to wash up.

The pain killer took effect quickly and he was already back to sleep before she left. At the office, she checked messages, checked e-mail, cleaned out the papers from the drop box and sorted them out. At eight she checked on the AC repair and found that no one would be available until Tuesday. She called Kevin, explained about the AC and asked if he would mind if she took a couple of days off. She told him that she would come in early and take care of messages and e-mails and take care of these issues from home as much as she could. Kevin agreed, she thanked him, scooped up the notes she had written. Locked up and left. On the way home, she stopped at the store to pick up a few groceries.

Karen J. Simon

# CHAPTER 8

The sound of closing doors penetrated the drug induced cloud that enveloped Trace in a floating world of tolerable discomfort. He seemed to rise and fall on successive waves of awareness, drifting in and out of blissfully pain free minutes. Time lost all meaning, day and night melted into one. A mirage figure with flowing red hair wove in and out of the mist, sometimes close enough to touch though he dared not try and sometimes close enough that he could feel her breath like a caress upon his skin. He moved his head. Sunlight blazed a golden path across the wooden floor. He was in bed. A strange bed. He lay still, listening. Doors closing. Music playing somewhere. A sudden breeze lifted the transparent yellow curtain. A door banged closed. Somewhere in the distance thunder rumbled.

Trace lifted his head and moaned softly as he started to roll onto his right side. Memory flooded back. He laid back down, waited for a moment and rolled to his left. His muscles ached and his body was stiff and sore, the pain in his ribs had lessened, but his skin still felt hot and raw. With an effort he pulled himself up to sit on the edge of the bed and then to his feet. Another roll of thunder rumbled, closer this time and another gust of wind lifted the curtain. A door was open near the window and a quick glance showed it opened into a full bath. He turned the shower on low, kicked out of his jeans and stepped into the flow of water. He winced as it touched his right side, so kept his body turned to keep the water on the left. Soap, shampoo, conditioner, razor and shave cream were lined up on a small shelf. His movements were slow and laborious, but at last he stepped clear, turned the water off and gingerly toweled his body dry. The shower had removed a few more drug cobwebs, but a combination of moist heat from the shower and residual drug effects gave him a sensation of rubber legs. When he stepped back into the bedroom, the sunlight had faded as clouds rolled across the sky. The curtain was billowing in the wind and thunder clapped loudly. Trace dropped the towel and used all of his strength to close the window. His bag was open on the chest at the foot of the bed. He removed clean jeans, slipped into them and headed for the door as lightening lit up the room and thunder crashed.

Into the kitchen through the living room and down the hall, he was alone. The back door was open and he watched as a bucket skittered across the drive ahead of the wind. A truck door slammed and footsteps ran toward the back step. Trace leaned against the hall door as Lee bounded in, pushing her windblown hair from her face. She stopped when she saw him.

"What are you doing up? How do you feel?'

"Sore. Stiff. Stupid. How long have I been here?"

"Well, now...let's see. It was Sunday when I took you to the ER. Now it's Thursday afternoon. I'd say you've been playing at Rip Van Winkle. Are you hungry? Best get your order in soon, I'd say we're gonna lose power before this one is over. How about some tomato soup. I just happen to have some made. It will take only a minute to warm and do you want coffee or milk?"

"You work this week? Please don't tell me that you took time off for this? Soup sounds good....and milk."

"Doctor said he didn't want you alone. Office AC didn't get fixed until Wednesday morning, so I just went in and checked phone and mail messages and handled everything from here. Do you still hurt a lot?"

"Still kinda numb. But I better sit down cause my legs feel like rubber."

"Here." Lee ran over and pulled a chair free as thunder rolled in to end in a roar almost over the roof top.

"Oh that one was close! Sit down, let me see if the soup is warm enough."

A cold wind swept through the back screen and as she hurried to close it, Lee shivered.

"Cold wind brings hail."

"Here?" He asked.

"Not necessarily right here, but cold wind always means hail somewhere close. How's the soup?"

The lights flickered, went out, came back on. Trace finished his soup and milk.

"I think I'll take that offer of coffee."

"Coming up." Lee cleaned up the kitchen and poured two cups. "Let's go to the living room. Can you get those candles off the table please?"

Trace got up slowly, picked up the candles and followed her into the living room. Curtains whipped out in the cold wind. Lightning flashed and thunder crashed. Lee set down her coffee and rushed to close windows, while Trace sat gingerly on the sofa. The first hail stones pelted the roof, tinkled against the windows. The storm closed about them with intense fury, wind and hail rattling window panes. Lightening split the sky, leaving the acrid aroma of sulfur while thunder embraced the house in rapid succession.

Lee curled up at the end of the sofa, pulling her knees up under her chin and hugging them tightly with her arms. Trace watched her.

"Nervous? Storm? Or Me?"

She met his gaze…locked eye to eye. "Both." She stated firmly.

"At this moment, you have more to worry from the storm. I'm pretty harmless, I'd say."

"There won't be much sleep as long as this keeps up. And I daresay, the fire crews will be called out. The heat spell was long and dry. Conditions are optimum for wildfire."

Trace closed his eyes for a moment and then a hand was on his, warm, even through the fabric of his jeans.

"Trace, let me help you back to bed. You've been dozing for a good hour. The main part of the storm has passed over. The thunder and lightning could go on for hours more."

He lifted his head and grinned at her.

"You're taking me to bed?" He asked wonderingly.

"No! Trace, I'm not taking you to bed! I'm taking you to your bed. Now! Come on! Up you go."

He stumbled to his feet and lurched toward the hallway, with Lee on his heels, her hand light upon his elbow. He had left the door open, the bed covers back. He sat down heavily and gasped as the shock went through his body, momentarily bringing him to full wakefulness. Lee pushed him gently and he sank back against the pillows, allowing her to swivel his body onto the bed. She slipped out and upstairs to change into her pajamas. Another storm moved in on the heels of the last one, rain pelting the windows, lightening further away and thunder rumbling in the distance. Lee went back into Trace's room and sat down on the foot of the bed. Watching and listening. Somewhere during the night she nodded and slid down to curl up at Trace's feet. When he stirred uneasily, she moved and reached up to touch his face and fell asleep again.

Trace woke with a start. He wasn't alone. He lifted his head and looked down in the darkness. Lee was stretched out at his side, carefully holding herself away from direct body contact. He smiled. A picture of innocence he hadn't expected to see in her. He didn't have the heart to wake her. He wanted her there. Wanted to reach out and touch her. He breathed in the soft fragrance of her perfume and felt the response in his body again. Drugs had done little to tame the need. Did he dare to take the risk his heart was moving toward? There was an air of self-reliance and self-confidence about her different than in most women he had been with or known. And yet, he found himself wanting to protect her in ways he hadn't ever wanted to protect anyone before. When he looked at her, he felt a softness deep inside of himself, a warmth that centered in his chest, in his belly that made him want to envelope her in his arms. He moved his right arm so that it made light contact against hers and closed his eyes.

The touch awakened Lee. She caught her breath and held it…listening. Was he awake? Asleep? His touch sent sensations down her arm to her belly. Tingling sensations radiated through her body. She wanted to pull away as much as she wanted to hold still. There was someone else in his life and she didn't want to encourage him into any type of involvement with her. She didn't want to be the healing balm that sent him back into the arms of another. She didn't want to be a casual fling. She couldn't let him see the effect he had on her. Allowing resolve to take over, she sighed and rolled onto her back.

Dawn was just beginning to light the eastern sky when she slid softly off the bed and tip toed out of the room. Soft as she had been, her movement woke Trace. He listened as she walked softly across the floor and out. Heard the sound of running water, the backdoor opening and closing and silence. Silence that went on so long, he pushed the covers off, and sat slowly on the edge of the bed. He padded barefoot through the house to the kitchen. Coffee was just completing its last chortling so he stopped long enough to pour himself a cup before stepping out onto the back porch. Soft tones of pink and gold touched the edges of the sky where dawn was breaking. Birds twittered and chirped in the trees and the song of a meadowlark warbled from somewhere in the meadow beyond the back sheds. The aroma of fresh washed earth and rain still hung in the air.

He leaned against a porch support, lifted his head and breathed deeply of the clean, fresh air. A shed door opened and Lee emerged carrying two bowls, still clad in cream and pale green colored flannel pajamas. Unaware of his presence, her attention was on the muted colors spreading across the sky. Half way up the path, she stopped, spread her arms out and tilting her head back, and still moving toward the house, turned slowly about as if embracing the dawn and the day. At the foot of the steps, she looked up, saw him standing there and stopped.

"Good morning," he greeted her and raising his cup, "and good coffee."

"Good," Lee said as she mounted the steps, "ready for that bacon and eggs, now?"

"Someone else stashed in the shed?" He asked, indicating the bowls she carried.

"An entire family!" She shot back.

"You have them on pretty short rations. How many are there?" Trace followed her into the kitchen.

"Five, counting mom." She glanced over her shoulder at him, dropped the bowls into the sink and turned for the hallway. "If you want to help, you can pour me a cup of coffee and get the bacon and eggs out of the fridge. I need to wash up."

When she returned, her cup was by the stove beside a package of bacon and a box of eggs. Two plates were on the table and Trace was just taking silverware out of a drawer.

"How are you feeling today?" She asked as she set a frying pan on the stove and reached over to open the bacon.

"Overall stiffness is pretty much gone, ribs are still sore, but I can breath and move a bit better. Skin is scabbed enough, but still tender. I don't think I need pain killers any more, nor do I think I should impose on your hospitality any more than I already have. You have been a gracious hostess…ah…a little rough at times…but I do appreciate everything you have done for me." He studied her movements, enjoying the sight she made preparing breakfast.

The aroma of frying bacon filled the kitchen. Lee kept her back to him. A stab of disappointment went through her when he mentioned leaving. She had gotten use to his presence, even liked taking care of him; then remembered that someone else was waiting for him to come home.

"Do you want to go into town when I go in?" The toast popped up and she reached for it at the same time he did. Their arms touched, she gasped and jerked away as if she had been burned. He removed the toast, set it on the plate, buttered it and put two more pieces in, suddenly aware of the tension between them.

By the time the second pieces of toast were ready, Lee was putting platters of eggs and bacon on the table. The first rays of the morning sun bathed the table in light as he set the plate of toast down. Preoccupied in her own thoughts, Lee turned...right into his arms...with a short shriek of surprise. Traced closed his arms around her. She looked up and her eyes met his, melting pools of green jade. He stopped thinking. He only knew that, at this moment, he wanted to kiss her, to taste her, to breath in her essence. And he couldn't stop himself.

His arms were bands of steel around her, firm, strong, the bare muscles of his chest a wall in front of her. When her eyes met his, she saw the flare of desire, knew what he intended to do and found herself powerless to stop him...didn't want to stop him. She was falling into the depths of his eyes, mesmerized by the raw emotion and need she both saw and felt.

Her lips were soft, sweet and what he intended to be just a light touch became much more. Her lips opened to receive his probing tongue, her hands flattened against his chest, her head tilted to allow him to take the kiss fully. And heat flared instantly. Like an exploding wildfire, it raged through her body engulfing him in its building flames. Her body moved against his and she felt his respond. There was no stopping the need rising inside of her. No stopping the hunger she had been unaware of. His hands slid down her back to her hips pulling her harder into him, moving her body against his, his thumbs pressing gently into and kneading the inside of her hips. His lips released hers and moved across her face, down to the tender skin of her neck. She moaned as his lips teased her skin, nibbling, nipping. Her belly turned with waves of sensations, fueled by the tingling radiating from her neck, rushing like a raging flood through her blood to her entire body. She ground her hips tighter against his hardness and he moaned, moving back to claim her mouth. His thumbs found the bare skin at her waist; she shuddered at the heat of his touch as he slid the soft material of her bottom pajamas lower. Her hands shook as she dropped them and desperately tugged at the snap on his jeans, wanting to feel the heat generated by his desire. As her fingertips brushed his naked skin, he released her lips, pressed his cheek against hers, his breath ragged and shuddering. She pushed his jeans down and wrapped her hand around his hardness. He groaned and claimed her mouth again; more fiercely as she released him, placed her hands over his and pushed her own pajamas down to feel his naked skin against her own. He lifted her to the edge of the table and she moved her legs to allow him access. His fingers moved from her hips across her belly and down, igniting every inch of her skin. Her body trembled in anticipation. Down into the soft folds of her womanhood and he found the wetness and moaned again as his fingers probed the source. She wrapped her arms around his neck, pulling him into a deeper kiss, her tongue seeking his, teasing his mouth. He pressed forward, feeling her lower wet moist lips open to receive him. She laced her fingers in his hair, pulling him deeper still until suddenly his tongue plunged into her mouth as he took a firm hold on her hips and plunged his hardness into the depths of her body.

She arched up to meet his thrust, pulling out of the kiss, dropping her head back to release the sounds of ecstasy rising from the center of her body. Release came for both of them in shuddering waves. She collapsed against his chest as he wrapped his arms around her and lowered his head to lay his cheek on the top of her head. He cradled her head in his hands, his fingers rubbing her scalp. The gasping stopped, her breathing slowed as the waves of sensation and pleasure receded.

Trace kissed the top of her head, rubbing his lips softly on her hair, breathing in the fresh clean smell. Lee opened her eyes and pushed him away from her. She slipped off the table, pulled up her pajamas and looked up at him.

"Damn you!" She whispered hoarsely and sped from the room.

Trace was stunned. He hadn't forced her into anything. Why was she angry with him? He bent to pull up his jeans and winced at the effort to stand. He hurried after Lee, calling her name. A door slammed upstairs and he stopped at the lower step, looking up before continuing to his room where he started the shower. He was just pulling on his clothes when he heard the back door and before he could get to the kitchen, her truck roared out of the driveway.

Lee was angry with herself and angry with Trace. Why did he have to be right behind her when she turned? She had fallen into his arms like a love sick school girl. And he hadn't stopped her! He had looked right into her eyes. Oh! Those eyes! Steel gray eyes that looked into her soul with the power to melt all of her resolve. What had happened? Her tummy flip flopped as her thoughts replayed the events at the kitchen table. Everything she didn't want! Why had she allowed it to happen? Her shoulders slumped forward. 'Because I wanted it to. Deep down it was what I wanted. I let it happen. It's as much my fault as his.' Her body had betrayed her. Had he known it would?

At the office, she turned on the computer and while it ran through its startup, she pulled a slip of paper forward to take messages off the answering machine.

"Good morning, Lee. Staying in today?" Robert Hadley, one of the rangers asked as he stepped in.

"What do you need?" She snapped.

"Good morning, Robert. How are you and what can I do for you? Who bit you this morning?" He threw over his shoulder as he walked out.

Lee rewound the messages. She hadn't heard one of them. There were four e-mails. She whipped out a short curt reply to one, sent an 'out of office' memo to one, jotted notes from the other two and set them in her 'IN' basket. The phone rang.

"Lee?" It was Kevin. "Are you all right?"

"Yes. Why?"

"Hadley just stopped by; he said something was up with you this morning. You bit his head off for saying good morning. Are you all right?"

"I'm fine Kevin. Can't a girl have a bad hair day for God's sake! Do I have to be cheery and smiley and happy all the time? I was up late, the power went off, the storm made me uneasy, I didn't sleep well, I didn't get breakfast, didn't get my coffee. I've just had a rough start. If there's nothing urgent you need, I'm going home and crawling into bed to see if I can find the right side to get out of next time!"

"Sounds like a good idea to me. See you on Monday?"

Half way home, Lee suddenly slammed on the brakes. What had she done? He was still there! His truck was at the motel. She would have to face him again. What was he thinking of her? Had he called his girlfriend? Told her that he was sorry for their misunderstanding and he wanted to come home? Well he had his healing therapy! And that's all he would get! By the time she stopped in the yard, she had regained her composure. But her legs felt like rubber as she stepped out of the truck and up the back steps. She scanned the kitchen, her gaze halting briefly on the table. Her cheeks burned at the memory of the mornings' events. The table was cleared, the dishes done and put away. There was no sign, no hint of what had happened there as the early morning sun lit the room. The room was still and as she walked through the house, she knew she wouldn't find him. She pushed open the door to the guest room, calling out before she stepped in. The covers were folded neatly back at the foot of the bed and his bag was closed atop the chest at the foot of the bed. She went to the back porch, scanning the distant meadow and saw no sign of him. She didn't recall passing him on the road, did not think she had been too preoccupied to have missed him. The large yard in front and the field beyond to the woods did not reveal him either. Once again, the house felt empty, a different empty. She walked slowly to the room across the hall from the one Trace had occupied – her father's old office - and dropped into the overstuffed leather chair that her father had loved. She buried her hands in her face, fighting back tears of disappointment, resentment and anger. He had even denied her a final angry outburst. Had denied her the right to accuse him of using her, overstepping the welcome she offered when he needed help, taking advantage of her.

Daylight faded from the room. Lee turned on a lamp and continued to work at the computer. The house remained deathly quiet. At last she turned off the computer and stopped at the door across the hall. His bag was still there. Where had he gone? Why had he left his bag? She walked to the bed and angrily tore the covers off, hugging the sheets to her as she took them to the laundry room. His scent still clung to the pillow cases, the sheets and she breathed in deeply, holding on to this last trace of him, wanting to savor one last time his maleness.

The house was a silent tomb all weekend. Late Sunday, she threw his bag into the truck and drove into town. His truck was still parked at the hotel. She went in to the desk and walked out stunned. He wasn't there. Hadn't come back, hadn't checked back in. What should they do with his truck? She didn't know. She'd get a hold of him and get back with them, she said. She drove home, feeling numb as she dragged his bag in and dumped it on the chest.

She called in sick on Monday and searched the sheds, the meadow and woods surrounding the house. There was no sign of him anywhere. He had just vanished. No doubt he had called his girlfriend and she had come to get him. They had taken a few days to go somewhere, to talk and settle their problems and rekindle their relationship. She buried herself in work at the office, working overtime because last weekends' storm had sparked a couple fires that had disrupted camping.

Just as she was getting ready to leave, Kevin stepped into her office.

"Lee, do you remember that guy that came in a couple of weeks ago? The one who wanted information on the mountain? Didn't you help him out? He wanted to spend some time up on the mountain, didn't he?"

"Yes. I remember him." She tried to keep her voice calm and impersonal as she replied. "I marked some maps for him. Why?"

"Sheriff called. Apparently he left his truck at the hotel. No doubt he'll be calling you. If he is up on the mountain we may to have to get involved in a search. You didn't drop him back off there did you? "

"No."

"Have a good weekend." He waved over his shoulder as he walked out.

The sheriff's car was parked at the house when she arrived and the sheriff was waiting on the back porch.

"Thought it would be best to do this out here. No one to see. No one to wonder why. How about a cup of coffee while we talk?"

"Sure." She said as she turned the key in the lock and stepped inside. The sheriff sat down and remained silent until she placed a fresh cup of coffee on the table in front of him.

"You know what this is about? The hotel called. Horn's truck seems to have been abandoned there. Wouldn't be so bad, except it's parked in front of one of their rooms. You spent some time with him, if I recall….we talked about it? Did you drop him off on the mountain?"

Lee sat down, rolling her finger around the rim of her cup, listening to his words. A short silence and she lifted her head to look at the sheriff.

"He went up on the mountain. I didn't go with him. But he fell up there and hurt himself. I took him to the hospital, they can tell you that. He took a pretty bad fall, scraped up his side and back, cracked a couple of ribs. Doctor didn't think he should be alone." She looked back down into her cup, swirling the cooling liquid.

"Then he's here?" The sheriff asked.

"No. It's not that easy Mr. Greer. He was here." She stressed 'was'. "But he's not now."

"Back up on the mountain? Lee, I gotta do something with his truck now that the hotel has called. Did he leave a key for you?"

"I don't know where he is, Mr. Greer." She set the cup down and dropped her hands into her lap. "I went in to work on Friday morning – I did every morning to make sure that everything was going all right there – and when I came home, he was gone."

"Do you know where he might be?"

"Well, he didn't say anything really. I had the impression there was a girl at home…and they…maybe…had a misunderstanding and this was cool down, rethink time. I guess he could have called her. I think maybe he did. I think they went to fix their problem – whatever it was."

"Well, I'll give him until Monday morning and then I'll send the tow truck over. One of you call me as soon as he shows up. OK? Thanks for the coffee."

When the sheriff left, Lee sat silent at the kitchen table. She almost hated it and the room. It only reminded her of his last morning here. She ran her fingers along the edge of the table.

"Why did you do this, Trace? I didn't even know you. I don't know you! I gave myself to you like a common tramp. You must really be enjoying the laugh on that one! Easy pickings in the mountains! I should hate you! And I want to! But somewhere inside, I feel something weird and odd, something soft and longing. I never felt like this. I never did that before. I shocked myself. I don't know what happened. I don't know how it did. I didn't know I could feel like that…react like that…respond like that. I didn't know anybody could make me feel that way. I can't help but wonder, Trace, do you make her feel like that?" She took a deep breath and pushed away.

Sunday morning passed. Just after noon, Lee went into the guest room and reached for Trace's bag. She didn't think he would be back in time and maybe he had left the key. She hesitated for a brief moment before pulling back the zipper. On top of his clothes was a white envelope with her name scrawled across it in neat crisp handwriting. She drew in a quick breath, recoiling from the bag and then reached out slowly to lift the envelope. She opened it and unfolded the single sheet of paper.

*Lee. I don't know how to say that I am sorry. I appreciate everything that you have done for me. Would you mind awful much moving my truck to the back of the hotel and give them the attached hundred dollar bill for parking? I hope that I haven't somehow hurt you. Please forgive me. Trace Horn.*

Cold. Impersonal. Should she have expected anything less? She picked up his bag, shoved the key and the bill into her pocket, threw the note into the garbage and went out to her truck. In town she took care of his truck, called the sheriff and then went home, tears streaming down her cheeks more from humiliation than hurt.

Two weeks later, she knew that she was pregnant, but she took several days off to drive into Sand Point to see a doctor and confirm it.

# CHAPTER 9

Rusty orange and bright yellow leaves rustled as a breeze lifted crisp edges and sent them skittering across the lawn. Late afternoon sun filtered through leaves still clinging to branches. Dark clouds on the western horizon gave promise of a gathering storm. Dishes clattered in a nearby kitchen and the aroma of charcoal drifted in from someone's back porch. Another unseasonably hot fall day that would end with the echo of thunder rolling across the open plains. A week of this weather had Trace on edge. He hadn't slept well last night and tonight didn't hold any better promise. The storm moved slowly, gathering force to break as the sun was sinking below the horizon. Dark clouds billowed high into the sky above town. Lightening forked across the sky with increasing intensity. On the horizon, sheet lightening shimmered, glowed and faded. Thunder began as a soft distant rumble and grew to terrifying crashes that shook the window panes in the old single story motel turned apartment house where Trace lived. Earlier, he had opened the window to get relief from the stifling heat that had choked the air in the tiny, close efficiency.

He threw himself onto the bed, watching the light dance across the expanse of sky visible through the wide window that looked out on the back of the building. The storm brought a rush of memories. He got up and went to the fridge, picked up a cold beer and set it back down, lifted a bottle of cold water and closed the fridge door then went to lean against the window, watching while his thoughts took flight.

The sound of Lee's truck faded and he was left in silence. He didn't know what had happened. One minute she was in his arms, soft, giving herself to him in an explosion of passion he had never experienced before. Then she had turned on him. He didn't know what had happened. He didn't know how it had happened. Only that it had. He hadn't intended to touch her, was startled when she turned…and was so close…Her eyes had burned into his, igniting a fire that exploded when their flesh touched. He couldn't have stopped if he had tried. He wanted her. He wanted to feel the heat of her passion, the taste of her kiss. He wanted to know every inch of her. All the things he had known were forbidden to him. But it hadn't stopped him from wanting, hadn't stopped the fire from burning out of control. He should have guessed how it would end when the first thoughts took root in his mind and heart and belly.

He knew he had no choice. He had to run. If she called it rape, he would find himself in real trouble. He had only one hope – that shame would keep her silent. He found a sheet of paper on the desk in her office, wrote a note and taped a hundred dollar bill for the hotel and the spare truck key to the bottom of it, placed it in an envelope and put it on the top of his clothes in his bag. He had put a few things into his backpack, slipped out the back door and hurried across the meadow heading for the mountain. He had to put as much distance between himself and town as he could in case Lee decided against him.

By darkness he had wound his way through the woods, roughly following the road up the mountain. He had stayed away from the road for the next few days, always working his way upward, camping early in secluded protected spots. By the second day, his body was stiff and sore again, the scabs had rubbed off the deep gashes and they had bled a bit, the healing skin was rubbed raw by the backpacks straps. By the third day, he had to stop and set up a better camp to rest and recover. He cut willows to make a crude lean to near a stream. Rolled a thin blanket out on more cut boughs, then stripped down to dip naked in the cold waters of the stream, allowing the water to cleanse and sooth the burning raw flesh. Then he rubbed ointment on as much area as he could, built a small fire and made willow bark tea. He spent two days there. Each day, naked from the waist up, he had made an ever increasing circle to explore the area. He had picked dandelion greens and fireweed plants, small button mushrooms and wild strawberries. He had cut them up in small pieces, chopped a small chunk of jerky and boiled them in water. Dehydrated survival packages at the bottom of his backpack could be stretched for a few more days by adding this to his meals.

For the next two weeks he had continued to move upward, stopping to repeat his circle explorations. He found two small groves of birch trees where bark had been stripped off. He found sturdy pines and mountain ash whose trunks had been notched or marked in some manner. In these places he made a place to sit where he could contemplate the terrain, smell the earth and the air and feel the ground and the surroundings.

He was worn and tired when he returned to town, deliberately making it in the wee hours of the night. He had spent the later part of that evening at the edge of the meadow near Lee's house, hoping to catch a glimpse of her. It was long past dark when he walked close to the gate. Light cast a warm glow through curtained windows, Lee's truck was parked at the side of the house. A door slammed and he wanted so much to see her...to talk to her. When he turned at last to walk away, a heavy feeling settled in his belly, weighing him down, slowing his steps. He walked to town and found that his truck had been parked at the rear of the hotel lot, his bag was on the front seat and the spare key on top of his clothes inside. No note. Nothing. A deep sense of disappointment washed over him. What had he hoped for? Just because she had found his note and done as he had asked didn't mean that she had any feelings for him. Apparently she hadn't called the law in. Maybe she had thought about it all. Maybe she wasn't as angry anymore. Almost without realizing it, he found that he had turned the truck toward Lee's end of town. There was no other traffic on the road. He turned the truck into the lane leading to the house and stopped. He couldn't drive in. He couldn't face her denial of him. He couldn't face her anger. He didn't want to hear her refusal, didn't want to see the rejection in her eyes. With a heavy heart, he turned around and drove out of town.

He hadn't gone anywhere, but he had driven as far as he could. He had no destination in mind. No place he wanted to go. He had no plans, no ideas. He had found his own peace and acceptance on the mountain and left his heart and soul at its base and the further he drove the more sure he was of that.

Lee's face haunted his sleep…he woke with the taste of her kisses still warm on his lips. He half expected to roll over and find her lying beside him when he awoke each morning. He could feel her hands on the muscles of his back…tingling the skin of his thighs. Whenever he thought of her arching her back to accept him, he felt a rush of heat that caused him to gasp for breath, longing to feel her warmth, her wetness, her heat. He couldn't escape the hunger, the need that hurt, that couldn't be satisfied or soothed.

The passing weeks hadn't eased the torture. Instead it had heightened his awareness of the lack in his life. It had built until he knew that he couldn't go on until he had faced the truth. He had to know in his heart what that was and he couldn't unless he faced Lee and talked to her. The one thing he hadn't been able to find peace with was her complete abandoned response to his touch. That, he was sure he hadn't imagined. How could she find him repulsive and still respond with so much passion? How could she hate him and open up to him so completely? How could she trust him enough to take him into her home and reject him at the same time?

He drifted into sleep as the storm passed over and began to fade into the distance.

"You cannot find peace when you run from life, my son. You cannot know the heart of another until you speak to them and look deep into their eyes. Look to the soul to see if they speak true words. The eyes are the windows of the soul – they do not lie. You look for answers where there is no one to answer but yourself. Why are you so eager to think that you know all? Did you learn nothing on the mountain? If you have left your heart there, your life can have no peace. A man must know and listen to his own heart if he is to have wisdom. To know your heart is to know your strength and your weakness. To follow it takes great courage. Your peace is on the mountain."

Trace woke suddenly. His heart thudded in his chest. The dream had been so real! He was sure he had heard his grandfather's voice as if he were sitting there in the room. He got up and realized that he was trembling. He sat down, trying to remember the words his grandfather had spoken in the dream, but they had faded into mist when he woke.

The light of dawn was muted and dulled by heavy clouds and drizzling rain. Trace showered and dressed, gulped down a glass of orange juice, grabbed his hat and coat and opened the door just as a red SUV stopped outside of his door. He slid into the passenger seat.

"Mornin, Ted. We stopping at Mickey's for a quick one through the drive up or are we eating at the Galley?"

"No time for either. I called Donny and told him to pick up to go's at the Galley. We have low ceiling today, scattered showers and maybe some rough air. You want to check the board to see if you got the Seattle/Anchorage seat? That should be posted this morning."

"OK I'll check that after I check the fuel sheets and load status. I assume you'll be watching the weather. How far does this extend?"

"All the way to Chicago and back. Coming in heavy again early afternoon with high cloud formations and possible winds up high. Probably make for a pretty rough ride home. But that may change by the time we head home. You know how this thing works!"

Ted reached over and turned up the radio and June Carter and Johnny Cash crooned "There will be peace in the valley…." before Ted turned the station and found John Denver singing "Take me home country road."

"I have a feeling it's gonna be an interesting day, Ted." Trace laughed. "I don't need to check the board, Ted, I got the bid. Look out Seattle! Here I come!"

"You sound pretty sure of that! You know there are some other guys bidding on that?"

"It's this thing called 'peace'. A funny thing my grandfather told me once. He said if you find peace around something, it's yours, so don't worry about it. I didn't know what he meant by that when I was a kid, but I think I may just be getting the idea."

The run to Chicago was not as bad as predicted and the return flight was pretty calm until they set back down at home, then the front moved back in, complete with night time tornado warnings. On his way through dispatch, Trace checked the board and found that he had won the Seattle/Anchorage seat. He would be expected to start in Seattle on November fifteenth. They were giving him plenty of time to give thirty day notice.

He gave notice the next day at the apartment and began making arrangements to close down local service accounts. It wouldn't take him long to pack.

The sky was heavy with the promise of snow when he drove out of town just after dawn on the third of November. Although he had planned to go to Salt Lake and over through the Columbia Gorge, the mountains of northwest Idaho drew him like a magnet draws metal shavings. He found himself in Boise and still headed north.

# CHAPTER 10

Lettie had decided to spend the winter in Georgia. Lee didn't know how to tell her mother about her pregnancy so had put off doing so. When the doctor had fist confirmed her worst fears, she had been overwhelmed with emotions, uncertainties, fears. She had made a serious mistake, but she didn't feel right in her heart about ending it. The doctor had told her it could be done and gave her all the information she would need. On the drive home, tears had run unchecked down her cheeks. She had cursed Trace with every breath and every mile. She had spent days agonizing over the ramifications of going through the pregnancy and keeping the baby and just as many over the heart rending decision of ending it all.

What she couldn't forget was the planting of the seed. It haunted her sleep, her dreams. Trace's eyes as he gazed into hers, before and during their moments of ecstasy. There had been no demands, no force…no roughness. He had touched her tenderly. He had held her afterwards, his cheek on her head…he had kissed the top of her head. There had been more tenderness in those few moments than she had thought possible. If she kept the baby, she kept that alive. She could treasure the feeling of total completeness that had enveloped her that morning. She would never lose the memory of it. It might fade, but she would always have this one thing, this one precious part of that day.

He must have made peace with his girlfriend, because he never came back...never tried to make contact. It had only been a quick summer fling for him; a release of his needs during the break in his relationship.

Was it like that for men? She wondered. Didn't they feel anything? Could they really go from woman to woman with no regret, no feelings, no remorse? Could they put so much into making love without meaning one bit of it?

She knew that she couldn't. No flesh to flesh contact had ever had so intense effect on her. No touch had ever excited her more nor flamed her passions to such a need for complete satisfaction. She doubted that she would ever meet anyone to match it.

How could she make her mother understand how she felt? And more, what would her mother think of her? What would she say to the boss? Would it change the way those at work dealt with her? She didn't form close relationships with co-workers. Everyone knew everyone else in this small town and everyone knew that she dated no one...that her life was wrapped up in her work, her mother and the disappearance of her father. There would surely be talk and questions about the unknown father. Was she truly ready to take on the role of a single mother, especially when there could be some adverse and negative impressions of who she truly was?

Then morning sickness hit with a vengeance. Kevin came in one morning in mid-August to find her weak and trembling between bouts of nausea. She had brushed it off as bad food. The second time, a week later, she had confessed to feeling under the weather, probably a touch of stomach flu.

Ten days later, Kevin had looked at her with sincere concern. "Have you been to the doctor, Lee? This has been going on for a little too long, don't you think?"

"I'll do that." She promised, but several days later, he told her that he wanted a doctor's note before she could come back to work.

"I went to the doctor, Kevin. I'm OK."

"What did the doctor say?"

"He said that I am fine."

"Good. Let me see a note to that effect. Until then, go home!" Kevin was emphatic as he headed for the door.

"Wait! Kevin. Can I talk to you?" She was weak and shaky, and she didn't know where to start or how to do this.

Kevin came back to stand in front of her desk. "Lee! Look at yourself! You're shaking like a leaf. I've never seen you like this! This has been going on for too long to be just a simple case of the flu. Did they run any tests at the doctors?"

"Yes, they did." She admitted slowly. "The doctor said this would go away. It's nothing to worry about. It should be easing off soon."

"What's wrong, Lee? Do you have an ulcer? Or is it more serious than that?"

"No, Kevin, it's not an ulcer and it's not serious. It's pretty common, actually. Look, I don't know what to say or how to talk to you about this, but I have to soon anyway. I have to face the music sooner or later and I need to start with you." She rushed on before he could interrupt, "I'm going to have a baby, and this is just morning sickness and the doctor said that it was normal and that it would go away and I asked him about working and he said it was OK and he said that I could work as long as I wanted to as long as everything was normal."

Kevin couldn't say anything for a moment, he was dumbfounded. Then finally only two words came out. "A baby?"

"Yes." Lee looked into Kevin's eyes and saw the shock and disbelief. She lowered her head in shame. "I know what everyone will think of me." She said softly. "If you want me to leave, I will."

"I can't make you do that, Lee, and you know it! But this does come as a shock. I didn't even know you were dating anyone - not that it's any of my business – but you've never brought anyone around, never talked about anyone – I don't think I've ever seen you with anyone, come to think of it. What you do with your life is your business, as long as it doesn't interfere with or affect your job here. When is the baby due? We'll have to start looking at how to cover some time anyway."

"March," she said softly, "and please, don't say anything yet. I need to figure out how to say this myself."

August was hot and muggy and frequently stormy. The heat sapped all of her energy and she didn't have much of that until the morning sickness eased off. The first part of September was unusually warm, but the evenings were cooler. Mid October brought the first hint of snow on the higher elevations. The trees were nearly devoid of leaves. They lay on the ground in a crisp multi-colored carpet that children and dogs found great delight in. Lee found that her clothes were getting a bit snug, so she shopped for one size larger and hoped to conceal her pregnancy for as long as she could. Kevin was still the only one she had talked to about it, but as the month drew to a close, she knew she couldn't keep it a secret much longer. Her belly was noticeably rounded while the rest of her remained slim and trim. She made regular trips to Sand Point, sometimes spending the weekend, so that it would appear as if she were seeing someone there. She mentioned her trips, dropping hints to give allusions of someone so that when the first comments came they included reference to it.

"Hey, Lee! Did you haul off and get married on us and not even invite us to the wedding or do we need to go have a discussion with someone?" The bantering was light and easy and she responded in kind.

"I told him I'm not ready, yet."

November came in with cold freezing rain and Lee looked forward to the first snow. She awoke early on the morning of the fifth to find the skies heavy with clouds that gave the first promise of snow on the lower elevations. It was Saturday and she stood on the back step looking out across the meadow to the mountain beyond. Behind her, the coffee pot gurgled and the toast popped up. She felt clumsy as she turned back in to take care of it, hearing the sound of a vehicle coming up the road and wondering who could be coming around so early. She buttered the toast quickly and took an extra cup from the cupboard as a door slammed and then turned as the knock sounded on the screen, the door opened and she stopped, holding the cups of coffee.

"Trace" she whispered hoarsely, "what are you doing here?"

He opened the door and stepped in, shock written all over his face. For one moment he had frozen as she turned. Dressed in dark blue sweat pants and an old white t-shirt, her swollen belly was all too evident.

Shaking, she walked to the table and set the cups down. Placing her hands on the table surface and looking down at them, caught unawares, she was not prepared to answer his questions.

"Lee?" He asked softly, the sound of her name filled with unasked questions. "I was passing through. I had to stop by. I had to see you. I just couldn't get you out of my mind, couldn't leave things the way they were. I had to clear things up – the right way. Can we talk?"

Lee pulled a chair out and sat down and without looking at him motioned across the table. But he didn't take a chair, he walked across to stand leaning against the cupboard opposite her. He glanced down the hall half expecting a man, her husband, to come walking in to join them.

"I hope my stopping by doesn't cause any problems? I guess maybe it was foolish, but I had to explain something to you. Not that it makes any difference now, anyway. But, when I came here last summer, I had just broken up with someone and I should have talked to you about it. I should have been up front with everything, but....I just didn't know how to."

Lee looked up at Trace...saw his glance down the hall and suddenly understood the nervousness. She wanted to tell him that her husband was sleeping, but she couldn't bring herself to lie.

"I suspected as much." She interrupted. "I should have been more careful. Let's just drop it. It's over and done with. I take it you made up?"

Trace looked closely at Lee. She looked away quickly. "No, we didn't. It was over before she left. I knew that when I came here. She was only part of the reason I came here in the first place. Most of the reason was me. I tried to tell you that several times, but I didn't know how to without offending you."

"Offending me?" Lee snapped. "You got what you wanted and you left without a word!"

"No! Lee, you did! You ran and you wouldn't talk to me...wouldn't give me a chance to talk then! Will you listen now? At least let's not part with hard feelings...." He paused. "You touched me, Lee. I could have..." He glanced quickly down the hall again. "Your husband is good to you?"

"My husband?" She asked and caught herself. "Oh, yes, my husband. Well…he…ah…"

"I better go. I just wanted you to understand why I hesitated in June…" He stopped again studying her. "Barbara couldn't deal with who I was…many people can't…and I was afraid you wouldn't either. I didn't want to hurt you by getting involved with you, but that isn't an issue anymore. Just…please…tell me that you forgive me for what happened?"

"Involved with me?" She asked weakly.

"I wanted to…then. I didn't want to embarrass you. Didn't know how to tell you that I was getting interested and that it wouldn't be good for you. I should have told you right away, but I didn't. At first I didn't see any reason to; it's always caused problems…being who I am; but I was attracted to you and for a moment I thought you were attracted as well and then I didn't know what to do and then you ran and I knew you didn't want anything to do with me. I'm sorry if I hurt you, I didn't want to do that and I wanted you to know it. I'd best get going, though, before I do cause problems for you." He glanced once more down the hallway, pushed away from the counter, still watching her, then walked past her and headed for the door.

Lee was trying to take in what he said. Trying to make it make sense. There was no woman? He hadn't gone off with a woman? Then where had he gone? She turned in the chair.

"Wait! Stop! If you weren't with a woman, who were you with? Where did you go for all that time? What did you do?"

He turned slowly and moved back to face her. "I went up on to the mountain - alone. I went to find a connection with my soul, with my past. I went to find peace within myself so that I could accept myself. In a small way, I went to find my grandfather. I guess I had some silly notion that I would find him there and that he would help me to find the peace I have longed for; that he would help me answer all of the questions that have hounded me all those past months. But he waited to come to me and it was too late."

"I don't understand." She said softly.

"There's no need to anymore. I hope you have found happiness. When is the baby due?"

"March." She said without thinking as he walked out of the door. She listened. The sound of a vehicle door, the engine and then tires on gravel. She turned back to the table, tears suddenly burning her eyes, running unchecked down her cheeks.

Karen J. Simon

# CHAPTER 11

The heavy gray skies seemed to weigh heavily on Trace's heart bearing down on his world. He went over and over the conversation he had just had with Lee. He kept seeing her standing in the kitchen, her swollen body proof of her new found happiness... her new life. He turned onto the main highway, stopped in town long enough to put gas in the truck and headed for the interstate. Miles slipped by, time slipped away, he didn't pay attention, he was so focused on the past summer. Thoughts and memories of the summer pushed aside any thoughts of the weather, the road, the new job, Seattle and life beyond this moment. Remembering how it had felt to hold Lee that morning. Remembering the sounds she made as she mounted to climax and the feeling of tenderness as she melted against him, spent. Remembering how it had felt to be inside of her, feeling her muscles contract around his hardness. She hadn't made any mention of a special man in her life. But then they really hadn't talked. He wondered if it was someone she had known a long time, someone she was seeing even last summer. Or was her husband someone she had met after he left. Her pregnancy was pretty advanced, so if it was somebody she met afterwards it had to have been really great. But then again, there had been no indication, really that she had any feelings for him.

"Damn!" He swore aloud. Why did it have to feel as if he had left a part of himself behind? Why had it taken him so long to accept that he cared about her…wanted her?

It was close to midnight when he pulled into Spokane and found a hotel room. He tossed and turned, unable to find enough peace from his tortured thoughts to allow sleep to claim him. With all too little sleep, he was up before dawn and on the road again. As he left Spokane behind, dawn was breaking the eastern sky and tiny snowflakes whirled and danced before a stiff breeze.

Once again miles and hours rolled by with thoughts tumbling around what was, what could have been and what could never be. The snow lessened and quit, but as he began the climb up the eastern slope of Snoqualmie Pass in the late evening hours, the skies once again opened. This time the wind was blowing the snow so hard it made driving more difficult, visibility dropped and, combined with low light conditions, the world outside became obscure and indistinct. By the time he topped the pass and headed down the western slope, complete darkness enveloped the truck. Somewhere ahead of him was Seattle and a new beginning.

*****

Lee called her mother two days after Trace left. She had put the news off long enough and so far she had been fortunate that none of her mother's friends had found out and beat her to breaking the news.

"Hello? Mama? How are you?"

"Oh, baby! I am so glad you called. Anna and I are going to Savanna for the holiday. We're leaving tomorrow afternoon and I was afraid that I would miss you and not be able to talk to you until after we get back. What are you doing for Thanksgiving, dear?"

"I don't know, Mama, I haven't decided yet. I may just stay home and enjoy the peace. It's been snowing and right now the roads are a bit slick. But Mama, I called to talk about something important and I don't really know where to start."

"Are you moving?"

"No, Mom. Not that easy and simple, I'm afraid."

"Are you leaving the Service, Lee? Or did you find something out?"

Lee laughed. "Well, Mom, sorta the last. But not what you think! I met a guy last summer and I liked him... a lot... too much... actually... and...I...wasn't careful."

"Lee! Is he going to marry you? What on earth are you going to do? Do you want me to come home?" Her mother was now anxious and worried.

"No, Mama. There's nothing you can do. And, no, he isn't going to marry me. He doesn't know about the baby because he left right afterwards. But I couldn't end it Mom, I just couldn't. So I've been going to Sand Point and spending time and everybody thinks there's a guy there..."

"When is the baby due?" Her mother asked. "How are you feeling? Did you have any problems with morning sickness? Why did you wait so long to tell me about this? And how are you going to take care of a baby all by yourself? Do you plan on getting a hold of him to let him know?"

"The baby is due in mid-March, Mom. I had some morning sickness, but it's all over now and I am feeling great…getting fat is all. You'll be home by May and we'll all be fine. We'll talk more about this later, Mom OK?"

"I'll change my plans! Come home in early March so I can be there when the baby is born! We'll just have to manage."

"Right now, Mama, I don't want you to change your plans. Let's just wait and see how things go, OK?"

When she hung up, Lee sighed. She had so dreaded that phone call. She knew her mother was disappointed in her. Knew that her Father would have been.

She wondered for a moment where Trace had gone. Just passing through, he had said. She kept repeating one phrase 'I was interested and I thought you were, too.' What did that mean? Did she dare put any meaning into it? He was interested? How? Had he wanted more than she had given him credit for? And if he had wanted more, why hadn't he said so? Nothing made sense. Had she misjudged him? Whatever had happened, it was over. She wouldn't see him again, she was sure of that. All she had to do was put him out of her mind and get on with living. But even as she thought it, she knew it was hopeless to think that she could do that with the child that had taken to kicking her so soundly; the child who would remain in her life – a constant reminder of the father who had helped create him...or her. She knew that she would never be able to look at the child without remembering that morning...Trace's lips playing across her skin, sending tingles along every tightly strung nerve to create sensations in every part of her body. His touch igniting every inch of her skin with burning flames that consumed her common sense and sent her into tremulous shaking wanting to climb to the highest peak before flinging herself into an abyss of breathless passion. When his fingers had touched the core of her heat, she had thought that there could be no more intensity to the sensations drowning her body and then his hardness had touched her, had moved slowly to enter her and she had soared even higher, wanting more, needing more to fill her until there was nothing left. Wave had cascaded after wave as they climbed to the final peak of sensuality and broke through the veil to achieve total consumption of each other. Weak and drained she had leaned against him, soaking up the warmth of his body, feeling the tenderness in his touch and kisses, wanting nothing more than to remain in the circle of his arms, locked in the embrace of his gentle love. But then she had remembered that he didn't love her, that he loved another. He had only used her to rekindle the flame of love, tenderness and passion for the woman he had argued with. Or had he? Suddenly she was confused. If it had all been real, what had she done? She hadn't given him a chance to tell her anything. She hadn't given him a chance to share anything with her. Instead, she had closed herself off from him, pushed him away and ran to wash it all off, run to put distance between them so that she wouldn't see the truth in his eyes when he looked at her. She collapsed in tears as she realized that she had run, he hadn't, at least not until after she had left no doubt that she wanted nothing to do with him. She couldn't change that; she wouldn't know where to look for him.

Lee spent Thanksgiving at home. Fresh snow was drifted across the lane, making driving difficult and hazardous. She spent Friday sorting through papers in her father's office, cleaning desk and file drawers. Saturday, she moved boxes to the attic and pushed two metal filing cabinets to the back porch. Sunday, after breakfast she found her old sled, maneuvered the file cabinets onto them and drug them to the storage shed at the back of the garage. By Monday the road had been plowed and she had no problem getting to work.

Kevin came in shortly after she arrived and dropped a box of Christmas decorations on her desk. "Joe Hudson and Gary Lepetski are coming by with a truck full of trees. I told them to make your office one of the first drops. When they get done, they'll be back to string up the outside lights. Think you can handle the tree? There'll be one tree left over – for your house – they'll drop it off when you're ready to go home."

Joe and Gary set the tree up in the front corner by the big window and left her to finish. She was just finishing the strands of tinsel when they returned to start hanging lights around the low eave of her office cabin. Before they left, they made arrangements to come by in the late afternoon to follow her home.

The tree they had selected for her home was tall and full. Once again they hauled it in and set it up. This one went in front of the huge plate glass window in the front room. She promised to call if she needed help with lights and the two rangers left.

The Christmas decorations were stacked in neat boxes in the closet in the downstairs guest room. It was the first time Lee had been in the room since removing Trace's bag. When light flooded the room, she couldn't help looking at the bed, the bed where she had fallen asleep next to Trace. She reached out to trace her fingers across the pillow case and thought of his dark head resting there. Thoughts of that week of tending him washed away thoughts of decorating trees and she sat down to let the tears wash down her cheeks.

Karen J. Simon

# CHAPTER 12

"Breathtaking, isn't it?" Wayne Gardner asked as the aircraft broke through the thick cloud cover they had flown above since an hour after departure from Seattle. "I've been doing this for the past five years and I never tire of the sight of those mountains; rugged, pristine, with glaciers that have flowed from their peaks for unknown ages. You get a sense of a land untouched by the hand of man, untamed, unreachable. Technically, this is the Pacific Coast Range that runs along the western coast of most of North America, but below us is a part known here as the Chugach Range. The highest peak in this range is about 13,000 feet. This range is also known to receive more snowfall than any other area in the world."

Trace looked out at an expanse of mountains that extended as far as the eye could see. Late afternoon sunlight had painted the lower slopes a deep purple that faded to various shades of purple, lavender and deep rose closer to the peaks where snow and ice reflected more muted colors. Breathtaking as it was, it also gave a sense of cold, unforgiving nature in its most raw state.

As the aircraft descended, Trace watched the unfolding scenery below him. Snow encased mountains, dark valleys, flowing glaciers and his thoughts went to another mountain and then, as always, to Lee. And again, he was struck with a deep ache of longing, a sense that he had left a part of himself behind when he left that mountain. A feeling he couldn't shake.

Snow blanketed the ground at Anchorage International Airport as the plane dropped towards the bluff at Earthquake Park, skimmed over the tree tops and settled onto the tarmac. In the right seat, Trace watched the scenery slip by, hoping to catch a glimpse of one of the moose that could often be seen in the trees along the runway.

"Dinner downtown, Trace?" The pilot, Wayne Gardner, asked as he brought the aircraft to a stop.

"Some place special in mind?" Trace returned.

"How about the Crow's Nest?" Wayne countered. "Great view. Been up there yet? On a clear day, you can see the Mountain. And the Sleeping Lady closer."

"The weather hasn't exactly been cooperating in that area. It's either been heavy overcast or dark. Most of the time we've eaten at the hotel."

"Most crews do that. I guess some get jaded about seeing places after so much travel. Not many like this run. Not many too enthused to get out and explore – after a while café food is just café food – Frisco's no different than Miami or Chicago or Dallas. I've been on this run for about five years and I like it. The Crow's Nest is a bit on the spendy side, but the food's great and the view is stupendous at any hour. We'll check in, change and take a cab over. You finish up here, I'll meet you in Ops."

Wayne stood, reached for his cap, picked up his brief case and stepped out of the cockpit. Trace went back to the clipboard and paperwork.

Forty five minutes later, Trace walked in to the Operations Center. Wayne was on the phone. Fred Moyer, the Operations Manager, was also on the phone, but he glanced up and lifted his hand in greeting. Cheryl Hyder, the pretty young native receptionist, had seen Trace coming and already had a cup of coffee ready to hand to him.

"Enjoy," she smiled and with a wave that took in both of the other men she added, "They're both going to be awhile. How was the flight today? I know, I already asked Wayne and he said that it was cloudy all the way up and a bit rough coming in here. But he says that all the time, so I don't know if he's telling me the truth or just repeating it all the time!"

Trace set his briefcase down, accepted the coffee and pushed his cap back on his head. "Can't answer for him all the time, but this time he was correct and to be perfectly honest with you, I have yet to see the mountains everyone says are there. The Alaska Range, right?

"No!" Cheryl exclaimed. "How long you been flying up here? The Alaska Range is north of us. You come over the Chugaches to come in here!" She shook her head and turned to answer the phone.

Trace smiled and winked at her. He picked up his brief case and found a seat in the crew lounge to wait for Wayne. He had nearly finished the coffee when Wayne opened the door. "Ready? I already called the hotel. Courtesy van should be waiting for us."

On the sixth floor of the Inlet Tower, Trace dropped his bag onto the bed and began shedding his uniform. Jeans, navy blue turtle neck pullover and a jacket and he was ready to go when Wayne knocked on his door and again informed him that the cab was already waiting down stairs.

A slender red haired waitress showed them to a window table facing the water when they arrived at the Crow's Nest. Trace stood a moment to drink in the twinkling lights of the city spread out below him. Wayne was right, the view was spectacular and suddenly Trace wished that Lee could see it, then wondered why that thought had crossed his mind.

"Could I get you gentlemen a drink while you wait for dinner?" The waitress asked. Trace shook his head, Wayne ordered a glass of red wine and the waitress disappeared.

"Somehow, I knew you'd like this." Wayne said, nodding at the view beyond the window. "You're not married." That was a statement more than a question as he continued, "Significant?" Without waiting for an answer, he went on. "Don't go hurrying into anything. Smart. Wish I could have talked my kid into that. Actually he's not my kid, he was seven when I married his Mom, but I raised him so I call him mine – along with his sister and the two boys we had. You know, I think that little Cheryl likes you. She's native, you know?"

"Meaning she was born here, right?" Trace asked over the rim of his glass.

"Cheryl is Aleut. She's from Cold Bay down on the Aleutian chain. Came to Anchorage to attend the University. Took a summer job in one of the airport gift shops and then got on here. She's been here since before I started coming in. Always got a smile and always friendly, but not so talkative. Don't think she's married, at least I never saw a ring on any fingers."

Trace laughed. "Trying to hook me up, old man?"

"Word's out that you're a bachelor on the prowl."

Again Trace laughed. "Didn't know I was…..on the prowl that is. Single, yes, and not that it's anybody's business, but I just got out of a relationship and not looking…at this moment."

The waitress arrived with the wine, refilled the water glasses and took their food order.

"Your wife doesn't mind you away from home on this flight?" Trace asked over dinner.

"We been married a long time, we're comfortable and secure with who we are and what we have. We've always talked on the phone about problems that come up and we always make time for us when I'm home. We don't hang on each other and smother each other. A lot of wives have to have their husband home all the time. I've never figured out if it's because they're insecure in themselves and their ability to be somewhat independent or if they are insecure in the relationship and strength of what a team can do...from anywhere. But being away from home isn't the only reason this isn't a popular run. A lot of guys just don't like this. It's too remote, it doesn't offer the same type of life that cities in the lower forty eight do. Some people view it as downright backwards and rugged and rough. I like it. I grew up in San Bernardino and I kinda like getting away from the rush and push of big city life. I like the laid back way of living I see typified here. They say you can find that in a lot of country areas and in the south, but its' different here. You travel much?"

"In the Air Force. I was all over Europe and the mid-East. I spent some time around Los Angeles when I was younger and I didn't like it then. I've hopped around some cities in the U.S. Didn't find anything I really liked."

"But you chose Seattle?"

"For two reasons - first I wanted to be back in the northwest and then – I just wanted to see this. I have a natural inclination toward the wilderness, you might say. I don't know, maybe I'm as unsettled as the country is."

"Sure you're not running from something?" Wayne questioned.

Those were the same words Lee had used. That he had heard from his grandfather in the dream. Were they right? In a way he was running. Away from memories of the few days he had spent with Lee, but mostly that last morning. And why, every time he flew over these mountains, did his thoughts go back to Ghost Cave Mountain? And why was he haunted with the feeling that he had left something very important on that mountain? He glanced out of the window, but his attention was caught by the reflection of the red haired waitress at a table behind him. Suddenly he noticed that there was something different about the way she was interacting with the three men at the table. He studied her reflection, her facial expressions, the stance and movement of her body and just as suddenly he heard his grandfather's voice… "The eyes are the windows of the soul…" The lights of the city were like a glittering carpet spread out before him, but the room faded and he was standing in the kitchen watching Lee. She wouldn't meet his eyes. He had thought that she didn't want to look at him because she was angry or because she couldn't deal with who he was. But what if that wasn't the case? What if he had projected that based on his past? Had she looked away because she didn't want him to see something else? She couldn't have faked the intensity of what he had experienced that morning six months before. Her eyes then had been focused on him, centered on him, climbing with him. He had gotten lost in the depths of passion reflected there and he had responded to it. Six months ago he had……he stopped and suddenly pushed his plate away. Why had he been so blind? Why hadn't he guessed? Why hadn't he just known? Why hadn't she told him?

He couldn't finish his meal. His stomach was slowly turning upside down. He glanced at his watch and did a quick time calculation. Too late to call and then he realized that he didn't have a number, but he could get it from Information. First thing in the morning, he decided.

"Something wrong with the food?" Wayne asked indicating Trace's plate.

"No. I guess I'm not as hungry as I thought."

Trace mentally counted minutes and the evening drug on forever, but at last he was closing his hotel door. He hurried to the phone, got an outside line and called Information in Idaho and jotted down the number the Operator repeated at his request. He would call first thing in the morning.

It was the first thing he did at six when he awoke for the umpteenth time. He held his breath waiting as the phone rang and rang. Maybe she had left for work already. He sat up, reached for a pen and the paper and called Information again. This time, he asked them to connect him right away, but once again, the phone rang with no answer. He tried after his shower with the same result. He ordered toast and coffee for breakfast in the hotel café, but had no appetite.

When he stepped outside, the air was crisp and cold and his breath hung as vapor in the air. The courtesy van was waiting and warm and somehow he managed to make small talk with Wayne as the van sped toward the airport. A light ground fog swirled among the trees along the shore by Earthquake Park, the water lost behind the veil that hung over the bay.

"This should clear by the time we take off." Wayne commented. "At least that's what ops said." By the time he and Wayne had walked out of Operations, Trace had tried a good eight or nine times to call Lee with no result.

This morning, he missed the moose that Wayne pointed out. He didn't see the Sleeping Lady and he didn't see the mountain beyond. The plane banked and turned toward the Chugach Range and he barely noticed the early morning sun painting the lower slopes visible below the high bank of clouds they were climbing into. His attention was on the instrument panel in front of him, Wayne's words and traffic control, but his thoughts were nagging him in another direction which meant he had to focus more on the task at hand.

When they broke through the cloud layer, Wayne turned on the autopilot and glanced over at Trace. "Preoccupied this morning? I couldn't get you to even look at the mountains!"

"Don't want to miss a thing going on here. And I could get lost looking at those mountains!"

Wayne nodded and picked up his thermos. "Want a cup?" He asked. "This cloud layer will probably last all the way to Seattle this time of year."

Bright sunlight slanted through the windshield as the two men drank coffee and talked, keeping an eye on the instruments as the miles slipped by below them. Before long, the aircraft dropped lower until it was slicing through towers of fluffy clouds, then it sank into the folds of soft clouds and broke out into drizzling rain.

*****

It was after one and the phone rang and rang. Trace closed his cell phone and turned the wipers up one more notch. He glanced at his watch, braked to a stop at the intersection, and flipped the cell phone again. He scrolled through his contact numbers until he came to Operations, then punched dial. The light changed, he checked both directions and shook his head as a car sped through the intersection against the red. As he turned into the apartment complex parking lot, his boss finally answered the phone.

"I hate to do this after being here only a short time, but I've just had an emergency come up." Trace hurried on before the boss could say anything. "Would it be possible for me to pass on my next flight? I have two days off starting tomorrow. I may need three or four?"

"It is busy, Trace, and we were planning on adding another flight day after tomorrow. Is there any way at all you can put this off a week?"

"I wish I could, but I've been on the phone since before I left Anchorage this morning, and I really need to attend to this."

"Alright, I can't argue against an emergency. I hope whatever it isn't really serious? Might just as well take off until the day after Christmas."

"Thank you, sir. I truly appreciate your understanding in this matter." Trace hurried through the rain to the door of his apartment. He grabbed two pairs of jeans, a sweater, his boots, and two pullovers and stuffed them into a nylon duffle bag. Socks and clean underwear followed. From the coat closet he took a winter coat and a pair of gloves. In the kitchen, he found a plastic bag and put in a half package of potato chips, the last two bananas, a peach and two cans of coke. A last check around the apartment and he dashed back through the rain to the truck, threw both bags on the front seat and backed out of the parking spot.

One last stop for gas and Trace turned onto Interstate 90 heading east. Rain turned into snow as he started up Snoqualmie Pass and by the time he began climbing the summit, the wind had picked up and snow swirled across the road reducing visibility and bringing traffic to a slow. Semis and a few smaller vehicles were pulled off to the side chaining up. Trace pulled over only long enough to engage four wheel drive. He stopped in Ellensburg to get a cup of coffee and see what the road ahead was like. More snow, more wind and some drifting, with low light making visibility difficult at this time of day.

Trace dialed Lee's number, but still there was no answer. If she had gone to work early this morning, she would have missed his earlier calls, but surely she would be home by now…unless she had stopped to do some shopping on the way home…or stopped to visit a friend. By the time he got to Spokane, she should be home. He made better time getting to Spokane than he had thought he would, but still there was no answer when he called Lee. He stopped at the Flying J Truck stop just west of town to put gas in the truck. He stepped into the café to fill his thermos with coffee and decided against waiting for food.

He had run out of the snowstorm west of Spokane, but as he passed through Sand Point and began into the mountains, it started again. When he left the freeway, there was less traffic and blowing snow accumulating on the road combined with reduced visibility once again slowed his progress. It was just after four in the morning and still dark when he pulled into Lee's yard. The house was dark, but her truck was parked by the side of the house, so he parked behind it, tipped his seat back and closed his eyes. Although he was tired, he slept fitfully, waking often, checking the sky and the house.

# CHAPTER 13

Shortly after six, a light came on in the kitchen; Trace sat up, grabbed his cap and opened the door. A light snow was still falling and his footsteps were the first to mark the snow to the back door. The amount of snow on the steps bore testament to the amount of snow that had fallen during the night. He kicked the snow off the steps as he mounted them to the back porch, pulled open the screen and knocked.

Lee wasn't feeling quite awake yet when she plugged in the coffee pot and dropped two pieces of bread into the toaster. So when the knock sounded on the door she stopped short. She hadn't heard any vehicles come into the yard and who would be here at this hour? She glanced out the window and saw her truck, and she could see the front of another parked behind hers. She moved slowly toward the door, it wasn't locked, but she took the knob and held it as she called out. "Who's there?"

"Lee? It's Trace. It's cold out here! Can I come in?"

"Trace?" She opened the door slowly and stepped aside as he entered. He was in uniform, a light jacket, dress shoes and dress cap.

"What are you doing here?" She asked as she closed the door. "At this hour?"

"I'm sorry, I tried to call you all day yesterday, but couldn't get a hold of you."

"I was in Sand Point." She explained as she moved to the cupboard to get cups and lift her toast from the toaster.

Trace moved with her, stopped her as she reached for the cupboard door and turned her to face him. He placed his hands firmly on her upper arms and looked into her eyes. "I need to talk to you. I need to ask some questions."

She looked away and tried to move but he held her. "I thought we had said all there was to say."

"Look at me." He said softly. She looked up to meet his eyes. "The baby. It's mine isn't it?"

She looked away quickly before he could read the fear in her eyes. "What makes you think that?" She asked trying to hold her voice steady and strong.

He moved one hand to turn her chin and lift her face. "We need to talk, Lee. About us. About me. About the baby."

"The baby is not your concern, Trace. It's not your business who the father is. Now, please, let me go."

"It is my business!" He said softly, "and so are you, because I care about you, very deeply and because I care about what happens to our baby. I care what happens to you and I care about what lies ahead for both of you."

"We'll be just fine!" She exclaimed and tried once more to pull away.

"No! It's not that easy, Lee."

As she looked up and met his eyes, he spoke, watching her. "Let me introduce myself. My name is Trace Little Horn. I'm Indian, Lee, and that makes the baby mixed!"

He didn't see what he had expected. There was no horror, no fear, no disgust. There was only determination…anger. "What difference does that make?" She demanded.

"I'm sorry, Lee. I never meant to hurt you. I was afraid of you…afraid for you and now I'm afraid for the baby and you."

She grasped his wrists and pushed. His hands dropped and she slipped past him. She reached out to touch the table and turned to him.

"The baby is mine, Trace. My concern…my worry. If you were by some thin chance the father, what difference would it make? So, you're Indian. I'm Scots/Irish with a little Swedish blend. What's the difference? What does that have to do with any of this?"

"It has everything to do with it, Lee! It's literally what started all of this in the first place!"

"I don't understand." She shook her head.

"Then let me explain what it's like to be Indian!" He said harshly. "I grew up with it, I lived it; I couldn't get away from it. My father died when I was very young and my mother remarried. My stepfather hated me and when my sister was born, he wouldn't let me near her and when he got drunk, he said awful things to my mother until she sent me away to live with my father's family. We lived on the reservation and I learned all about being Indian. When I joined the Air Force I thought I escaped it, but then Barbara found out and she said she deserved far better when she slammed out. That's when I came here." His voice dropped as he slumped back against the counter. "I didn't know who I was. I hated who I was. I didn't understand a lot about life or about me." He paused and in the silence he looked down at the floor searching for the right words to go on. When he looked up again, Lee was sitting, watching him. "I didn't tell you because it didn't matter and then I couldn't find the right way or time to tell you and I was afraid that you would hate me. And then…that morning…Oh, Lee, I'm so sorry! I don't know what happened. I wanted to kiss you. I wanted to hold you. I wanted to make love to you. And I wanted you to want the same in the worst way. I just didn't think I could bear for you to tell me to go away. And then I couldn't stop myself…and you responded like dry grass to a hot match. And when you left, I was afraid that you hated me and I couldn't bear to see the hate in your eyes, so I went to the mountain to find peace…to find some comfort for what I had done…to come to some understanding of who I was…and when I came back…I was so afraid to see you…I had to get away…but I took you with me and I couldn't escape you…so I had to come back…."

Lee shook her head. "This isn't making sense, Trace."

"I know. I guess…what I'm trying to say, Lee…is…that…you…you…got to me. I can't stop thinking about you…about that morning…about holding you. I guess what...I'm trying to say is...I think I'm in love with you and I know that isn't even right! I want to be with you. I want you to be with me. But as much as I want it, it scares the hell out of me!" He pushed away from the counter and moved toward the table, pulled another chair, placed it in front of Lee and sat down. "The baby is mine, too, Lee...part of me...which means he has to face the same things I have. And you will, too...for having a breed." He reached out to take her hand and his voice softened. "I want to make it right, Lee. I'd like to ask you to marry me, but I won't ask you to do something you don't want to do. I want to help you through this; I want to be there for you and for our baby."

"You ran because you're an Indian?" Lee stood up, shaking her head and moved slowly around the room. "Why?"

"I told you, Lee, a lifetime of being labeled, of being pushed away, of being made to feel ashamed of being who I was, what I am." He stood up and went back to lean against the counter. "I didn't want you to know that. Lee. Stop. Please. Just answer one question for me."

Lee stopped to fill a cup with fresh coffee. "Why did you come back then? What do you want from me?"

"I came back because I care about you, haven't you heard anything I said? But I need to know; that morning... you responded... You didn't feel... Did... Did you feel anything?"

She sipped coffee, watching Trace.

"Trace, I knew your heritage the first time you stepped into my office. When was the last time you slept?" She turned to pour a second cup of coffee and walked across to hand it to him. She looked up to meet his gaze and held it, searching his eyes as he looked into hers.

"I don't think we're going to get anywhere at this rate. So let's start all over, shall we? And let's start back in June. You stepped up behind me. I turned right into your arms. And you…"

"Took advantage of you." He finished for her. "I got lost in the moment. I had thought about touching you…holding you…and suddenly it was happening. I didn't really have any intentions of doing that…We were both putting stuff on the table…I didn't realize that you would end up where you did."

"I couldn't get away…"

"Did you want to?"

"No." She said softly. "I had the same thoughts."

"So I didn't imagine your response?"

"No." She repeated.

"Then why did you leave?" He sipped coffee, watching her over the rim of the cup.

"I knew there was a woman. I thought that you were using me to return to her…to rekindle your feelings for her…to make things right so you could go back and put your relationship back together."

"How did you know about Barbara?"

"I didn't really, I just had the impression that you were running from something and a woman was the only thing I could see you running from. I was angry that you would use me like that!"

"Barbara thought I was Italian. She found out that I was Indian. Italian was romantic. Indian was savage. Italian was fine wine and good food. Indian was whiskey and poverty. Italian came with a great lineage and class and heritage and blood lines. Indian came with no roots, no background, no knowledge, no civilization, no art, no culture. Indian was disgusting, dirty, filthy, uncivilized, savage, inhuman. She wanted no part of it. She was a business manager at a financial corporation. We met at a Christmas party. She was attracted to the uniform and the pilot. We lived together for two years. She didn't want to get married right away. She walked out…six months before I came out here. Six months I hated myself…couldn't look in the mirror without seeing a savage. Same thing my stepdad called me. I wasn't running from Barbara, I was running from me. After I met you, I never thought of her again."

"Then why did you leave?"

"I was afraid of you. I didn't know why you ran. Didn't know what you would do after you thought about it. I didn't want to hear you say the same things she said. The only place I felt safe was going to that mountain. Do you remember when I told you that my family lived in this area? My people lived on the mountain and all around it. My grandfather was born in a tepee in a mountain meadow. He took me there when I was little; I wish I could find that meadow. My grandfather tried to tell me that our people were a proud people and I should be proud to be one of them. I wanted to find the same peace that he carried with him. I wanted to know why he could be so proud of being an Indian. I wanted to feel the land as he had and I felt the only place I could find that was the place my grandfather talked so much about. I wanted to touch the soul of the mountain and feel the pulse of my people. Somehow, I felt that if I could do that, I would breathe in the knowledge, the heritage, the culture and I would know better who I was and what my worth was. If I walked where generations of my family had walked, I would feel more at home, I would find acceptance of who I am."

"Did you?"

"In some small way, maybe. It was almost like a vision quest. I came away with a new respect for nature and the land. I knew why my grandfather could feel such peace, because it is the only thing there is all over the mountain. Silence and acceptance. If you are still and silent, you can see the beauty of life, because it comes to life all around you. But I found a part of what I was looking for right here at this kitchen table. I just didn't accept it for a long time. I wanted to deny what was in front of me that day. I wanted to deny the whole experience, because to accept it…to embrace it completely meant giving up a life time of internal conflict and low self-esteem. It meant living a full life…being happy…being loved…being accepted…being a part of life…giving and receiving. I found a great measure of peace right here and I left it that morning and carried the loss of it aching inside of me without truly understanding. But I had to find it again. I had to see if it was real."

"And what did you find in this kitchen?"

"You…and what you have to offer."

"You came back and left again."

"Yes. My grandfather told me that I would find no peace in running; that truth was in the heart. I had to know if you felt the same way I did that morning. But you were pregnant and I thought there was someone else and I didn't want to interfere."

"What brought you back?"

"A couple of days ago, I went with Wayne to dinner at the Crow's Nest in Anchorage. I watched the reflection of our redheaded waitress in the window and I heard my grandfather talking about the soul being reflected in the eyes and I remembered that when I was here you wouldn't look at me. That's when I knew that the baby was mine. I couldn't believe that I had been so blind. I couldn't understand why you did not tell me, though."

"Because you ran…because I was afraid that I had been used. Because I thought there was someone else in your life. I didn't want to interfere where you obviously had no interest."

"No interest! Lee! How could you think that after that morning? Did you think I do that with every woman I meet? Was there no feeling…no emotion…shared and given that morning?"

"I thought about every moment of that morning…relived them…searching for something that might tell me there was none. But, like you, I denied that it was there. To see it and accept it meant knowing you cared. And I didn't want to admit the possibility of that."

Trace set the coffee cup aside and reached out to touch Lee's face with his fingers. "Is there a possibility of exploring the feelings of that day? Is there a chance for you and me?"

Lee searched his eyes as his fingers played across her cheek. "I wanted you before that day. I wanted to know how it would feel if you put your arms around me. I liked the sensations you sent through me. I want to feel that again."

"I drove all night long to hear those words, Lee. And every mile was worth it." He leaned forward and touched his lips to hers, lightly, then breathed across her cheek to whisper, "Natalie McDougal, I love you! And I want very much to make love to you again."

"That's a little difficult, right now, Trace Little Horn," she said breathlessly, "there's a baby between us! And we have a lot to talk about if this is going to happen."

Lee stepped back, still looking into Trace's eyes. "First, I have to talk to my mother."

"Right now?" Trace asked.

"In due time," She replied, "right now, there are more important questions. When did you sleep? When did you eat? Where did you drive from?"

"I left Seattle yesterday afternoon just after one. I ate a peach at three this morning and I caught some catnaps in your driveway waiting for you to get up."

"The last thing you need is more coffee. The bed is made up in your old room. The sun won't be up for a couple of more hours, so why don't you go get some sleep. I've got to work today. Will you still be here when I get home?"

"Can I bring my bag in?" He asked.

"I've got to get a shower. Make yourself at home."

She watched him walk out the door before she headed upstairs. When she heard the sound of his truck, she looked out to see him backing away from hers and she waited for the sound of the back door before she stepped into the shower.

*****

Trace dropped his bags on the chest at the foot of the bed and was asleep almost as soon as he lay down. He didn't hear Lee open the door to peek in on him and he didn't hear her leave. He wasn't sure what woke him, but he lay listening. He wasn't sure how long he'd been asleep. He rolled over, turned on the light and looked at his watch. Two thirty five. He slid off the bed, running his hands through his hair and walked through the silent house.

Outside, snow was still falling. The clouds seemed to have sunk lower to the ground, bringing an early dusk. Across the fields, the trees were only a dark shape through the thickening snow. Wind picked up snow and tossed it airborne. In the front of the house, Trace's truck was a dark shadow disappearing under a thick blanket of snow.

In the living room, Trace bent over to plug in the tree lights and smiled as the tiny bulbs brought a soft glow to the room. The tree reached nearly to the ceiling with an old fashioned spun glass angel on top. A white cloth with silver threads was wrapped around the base of the tree. Several packages wrapped in colorful paper were set at the edge of the cloth in a semi-circle. There was still time to shop and add a few more, but first he wanted a shower and clean clothes.

Showered and dressed he returned to the window. Wind driven snow pelted the window and swirled around corners as gusts picked it up. Drifts were forming in the yard and fields beyond. This storm now had all the earmarks of a healthy blizzard and Trace wondered if Lee was still at work. He found his phone and called information to get the number for the local office of the Forrest Service. When he got through to the Operator, he asked for Lee McDougal's office.

"Most of the offices closed over an hour ago." The Operator responded. "Nearly everyone left when road condition warnings were sent out. I can try for you, but I doubt she's in, she lives out of town and I'm sure she'd want to get home before the roads become impassable."

Trace hung up, looked at his watch. Unless Lee had stopped at the store, she should be home, but surely she wouldn't linger too long if the roads were expected to get bad. Forty five minutes passed and Lee was still not home. Daylight was fading fast, the wind had come up even more and snow still fell heavily. The trees across the field were hidden behind a veil of snow and the front gate was a dark shadow.

Trace went to his room to get his heavier coat and gloves and then searched until he found a broom in the pantry. Wind driven snow stung his face as he stepped out onto the back porch. He pulled the coat collar up and moved away from the door. The steps were buried under drifted snow and drifts had begun to form across the drive. Trace brushed snow away from the door of his truck, opened the door and reached in to turn the ignition before attacking the snow that had completely covered the windshield and hood. When he finished, he stuck the broom into the snow, brush up and kicked snow off his boots as he stepped up into the truck and reached down to engage four wheel drive. For one brief moment there was a hesitation before the wheels turned and dug into the snow as he gently applied pressure to the accelerator. Slowly he maneuvered the truck towards the main gate. Once into the tree protected lane, the snow wasn't as deep and moving was easier. By the time he cleared the tree lined lane, darkness had descended across the land. Blizzard conditions obliterated moon and stars. The head beams of the truck stabbed the darkness ahead, but visibility was reduced further by blinding blowing snow and the truck was reduced to a creeping pace. Trace wasn't even sure he was on the road until suddenly a faint red light appeared in front of the truck and then a dark form in front of him.

Lee's truck was sideways across the road directly ahead and it was the tail light he had seen. He brought his own truck to a stop within inches of the side of Lee's. He opened the door and leapt into the snow, plodding as quickly as he could around the back and up to the driver's door. The door opened and Lee turned to him as he reached out to pull her to him.

"My God, Lee! Are you all right? What happened? How long have you been here? I've been worried about you. I called the office and they said you left hours ago."

"I did leave early, but I stopped at the grocery store, the mall and the post office. And then I just took my time driving. The wind has some pretty solid drifts across the road and I didn't want to get stuck or flip the truck over. Visibility kept getting worse and worse and I drove slower and slower to compensate and I really wasn't sure exactly where I was. I was so relieved when I found the road, but the drifts in here have packed harder and the truck slid sideways between two deep ones."

"Let's get you into my truck. We won't worry about yours tonight." He helped her out of the truck and back to his, then transferred her packages and turned off the ignition, leaving the hazards flashing.

Slowly and carefully, Trace backed his truck staying in the same tracks he had made coming out. When he reached the relative protection of the trees where the wind had been unable to drift the snow as deeply, he managed to get the truck turned around and continued back to the house.

Safe at home, Lee dropped her coat onto the back of a kitchen chair and began making coffee while Trace brought in the bags from the truck and set them on the table. With the last one inside, he shrugged out of his coat and hung it over Lee's. The aroma of fresh made coffee filled the kitchen.

"There's some Kentucky Fried chicken in one of those bags." Lee said over her shoulder as she reached up to open a cupboard door for plates. "Do you want to set the table or empty the bags?"

She turned…..right into Trace's arms.

"First, I want to know that you are really OK. Lee, I was worried about you. Are you sure you are up to doing all of this right now?" His hands rested lightly on her shoulders as he gazed down into her eyes.

Lee held his gaze for a moment before looking back at the plates she now held pressed against his chest. She said nothing and refused to look back up. Trace dropped his hands and stepped back, allowing her to move past him to the table. In silence he reached into the bags, handing contents to Lee to put away, until she swept past him to scoop up the last bags and hurried out of the room.

Minutes ticked away. Trace poured coffee, set the plates out and began opening food containers of chicken, mashed potatoes, gravy, biscuits and coleslaw. He leaned back against the sink watching the door to the living room, drinking his coffee, waiting.

When Lee reappeared, she avoided his eyes, moved to the table and pulled a chair. Trace sat opposite her as she served up the food and they ate in silence. When the table was cleared, Lee poured a second cup of coffee and sat down.

"Did you sleep?" She asked as he sat across from her.

"Mmhhmm. And after your day, you must be exhausted."

"Mmm…not really. I think we need to talk."

"Ask, Lee. Anything."

"At this moment, Trace, somehow, I don't feel like I know you; who you are; anything. I am still so confused."

"I know. I am in many ways a total stranger. I came into your life and left it with little notice. We had some major misunderstandings and they need to be clarified. When I left here last summer, I was running scared. I was afraid that you saw me as Barbara did. I was afraid you would think I took advantage of you and that you would take steps to protect yourself from an Indian. I came back by here before I left. I wanted to see you…to talk to you…..I just couldn't get past the fear of rejection – I didn't want to hear it…see it in your eyes…..but I haven't stopped thinking about you…about what happened between us. At first I got as far away as I could. First Montana, then Wyoming and Colorado. Then I got a job out of Seattle because it brought me closer to you and where we met and I stopped by on my way and…..and….I thought you were married and I ran again…..But there has been no peace even with all of that… I had to know for sure. When I knew the baby was mine, I knew I had to face you…had to have answers…know the truth…no matter what it was……."

"I suppose I need to take a share for all of this mess. When we first met, you hesitated when I asked if you were involved. I jumped to the conclusion that there was someone in your life, that you two had argued and were working out problems and that I was just a pawn in the game until that was accomplished. I never asked more questions. I should have. I was attracted to you. I didn't want to know there was someone else. I gave in to my own hunger for you and I was angry at myself. I didn't realize the depth of my feelings for you until after you had gone. I didn't give you a chance when you came by again – by then I wanted to hurt you....I wanted you to go away quickly before I changed my mind and weakened again. I knew I loved you, but I didn't want to love you and I didn't want to admit to myself that I loved you so much. But with all of that said, Trace, I am reluctant to jump quickly."

"I understand that. I don't want you to. What I want is for you to know that I love you, that I care what happens to you, that I want to be a part of your life...if you will allow me to. If you have any doubts...problems...because of...what I am...I understand that, too. If that is the case, though, please be honest enough to put it into those words. You tell me what you want from me and we'll work this out. If you want me to leave, I will as soon as the storm is over, though I don't think it wise you stay here alone. Is your Mother coming?"

"Who and what you are...being Indian is no concern for me. There are lots of people who neither see nor care about those issues. I knew your heritage in the beginning. It had nothing to do with what happened inside of me. You had everything to do with it. I have never felt like that before. Never reacted like that before. Is it real? Is it a girlish crush? I need to know for sure. Mom is not due back until May."

"But the baby is due in March? How do you plan to handle that alone?"

"I've been going to the doctor in Sand Point. I'll work as long as I can. When it gets close I'll get a room in Sand Point until the baby is born and then come home. I have a month or so off and then Mom will be here."

"I'm flying out of Seattle. I have to be back at work after Christmas. Can I stay? Can I help? I can look into a transfer. I want to be here with you…..for you……"

Lee turned the cup slowly in her hands as tears stung her eyes. This was what she wanted…had wanted ever since she knew she was in love with him. But could she ask him to give up his life for hers? Could she pack up and leave the mountain? And what about her mother? She looked up ……………into his eyes……

"How can I ask you to give up your job?"

"You're not. I can fly out of Spokane or Boise or Missoula. I don't need to fly out of Seattle. I'm a good pilot. I work hard and honest. I can ask for a transfer. I don't really care where I am as long as you're there. In many ways this country is more home than any other place I've been. Look, Lee, I don't want to push you…to rush you into anything you're not comfortable with. I want to spend this time getting to know you better, loving you, being with you, sharing. I want you to be comfortable with me, loving me, being with me. Let's do this slow. We have til after Christmas. There's plenty of time to talk about what comes next. It's Friday. We have the weekend. Monday is Christmas Eve. I don't have to leave until Wednesday. You want to talk to your mother before we go any further?"

"Not tonight." Lee pushed the cup away. "Tomorrow." She looked at him as she pushed away from the table. "Do you like Christmas?"

"I've not taken time for it since I was a kid. I don't remember the early ones and Mom made them for me after she married. My grandfather liked the holiday lights. We did very little, but we were close. I like your tree...the way it's decorated...the way the lights soften the living room...the way they glowed through the frosted windows and the falling snow. Being with you makes it all different."

"Well, the guys at work got the tree in for me. I couldn't have done it alone. Christmas was always special with my parents. Different without Dad...sad...lonely...and Mom missed him then as much as I. But...." Her eyes twinkled as she looked at him and stood up. "...I think I'm looking forward to this one. Shall we?" She reached out her hand. He took it as he stood. She turned off the kitchen light and they stepped into the softly lit living room and moved to stand by the tree where she indicated the few wrapped gifts. "I got some for the baby and some for Mom." She turned and he reached out to touch her cheek.

"I want this Christmas to be special – for you." He said huskily and leaned forward to brush his lips across her forehead.

For one brief moment she relaxed, allowed his lips to linger, then she pulled away, reached out to touch a bit of tinsel, then stepped toward the couch where she moved several small throw pillows and settled into the end seat. Trace remained at the tree watching her every movement.

"Lee, you don't believe any of this, do you?"

"I'm trying to Trace. There's so much to take in, to sift through and at this time my emotions are already in hormonal whirls. You talk of issues that had tremendous impact on what happened between us. They're foreign to me. I was raised in such an accepting, nonjudgmental environment. They are issues that never occurred to me to even take into consideration. I can very well see that there are portions of this that I gave to...that I had some real part in the misunderstanding... I don't even understand why...except that I was foundering in emotions I had never experienced before and I was afraid of the same rejection you feared. And to find out that we both created a horrible misunderstanding that has resulted in so much hurt is something to deal with. I'm not sure how to do this."

Trace sank onto the couch and reached for her hands.

"Lee. Don't over analyze this. We've both admitted mistakes. We've both admitted feelings. Let's start with that. Help me to accept your love for me... your acceptance of who and what I am. And I'll help you accept that I truly care for you...want you...and our baby. I want to be here. Why else would I be here now? What else could bring me back here? I'm not asking to pick up where we left off that morning. I'm only asking for a chance to change what we created in our misunderstanding of each other. Let's put the past behind us for a few days and start over. Tell me about Christmas for you in the past – with your family."

His hands folded hers in warmth. She watched his fingers wrap around hers, felt the tingling sensation deep within her that his touch had first created last summer. She raised her eyes to look deep into his dark eyes.

"Christmas was always so special. Dad went out for the tree while Mom and I made cookies and hot chocolate and sorted through boxes of decorations. He'd come in dragging snow and pine needles and we all planned the setup, strung the lights and hung the bulbs and tinsel. I went with him a few times in my mid-teens – sometimes we had spotted the tree during the summer. Christmas music on the radio. Mom loved to sing along. Secrets. Presents. Christmas Day we opened gifts together, talked, cooked, ate. It was just precious close family time and I missed it so much this year with the guys from the office bringing the tree and all and mom being gone."

"Well, you have the tree…the decorations…and we have time to shop for more gifts as soon as this storm lets up. Did you have plans for Christmas?"

Lee smiled. "I had plenty of invitations, but I hadn't accepted any. I didn't want to be obligated in case I didn't feel up to it when it came around so I left them all open. I got a small ham for dinner, but if you want traditional, we'll have to do more shopping. What kinds of food would you like?"

"Well, Christmas dinner just should include turkey, stuffing, potatoes and gravy - for a start. Yams with marshmallows, creamed corn, cranberries, pickles, warm homemade baking soda biscuits, apple pie, warm spiced cider…."

"Whoa!! Are you volunteering to make the biscuits? And Apple pie? And warm spiced cider?"

"Well… you did ask… look, I'll make a list tomorrow and help with the shopping and cooking if you make a list of what you want. I think if we work together we can come up with a meal to last a week. What do you think?"

"I think it's time to turn in. I guess I am tired. More than I had thought."

Trace stood quickly. "Are you alright? Can I do something?"

Lee accepted his hands and pulled up from the couch "I'm fine. It's just been a long day with a lot happening. There are towels in the guest bathroom. If you need anything let me know. I'm going to draw a warm bath before I turn in. Would you mind turning out the tree lights?"

Trace watched as Lee mounted the stairs then turned to the tree. With the lights out, he stopped at the front window and looked out. Snow fell thickly, driven by the wind as a thick curtain across the yard, obscuring the world beyond.

At the top of the stairs, Lee turned and for a moment her eyes lingered on the scene below. A sense of peace and belonging pervaded the room. Trace looked so right there, standing by the window looking out. There was comfort knowing that he was here, that he wanted to be here…wanted to be with her…and the baby. She smiled, smoothed her hand across her swollen stomach and whispered softly, "Honey, your daddy's here and, somehow, I feel like everything is going to work out fine."

# CHAPTER 14

Trace rolled over, opening his eyes and adjusting to the darkness in the room. The house was quiet and still, the wind had ceased it's howling outside. A shaft of light came through the curtained window laying a pattern across the floor. How many nights had he lain here in this bed while his body mended? He pushed aside the covers, slipped out of bed and went to the window. Snow was still falling, but the wind had stopped, allowing the snow to drift lazily down from the sky.

A door closed and Trace turned quickly, reaching for his pants. The tree lights were on and so were the kitchen lights when he entered the living room. The coffee pot burbled softly but there was no sign of Lee. Trace turned to glance back into the living room then heard sounds on the back step. He opened the door. Lee was on the porch with a broom brushing snow off the steps.

"What on earth are you doing, Lee?"

Startled, Lee looked up. She stopped, setting the broom aside and extended her hand. "Come here." She said softly.

Trace took her hand and allowed her to lead him to the end of the porch. The scene beyond glistened in the light cast by the yard light. Huge snowflakes shimmered against the darkness beyond as they drifted softly out of the sky, settling onto the surface of everything in puffy piles. The only sound was the soft shushing of the snow flakes.

"Its breath taking, Lee!" Trace whispered, pulling her against him.

"It's a memory moment." Lee murmured.

"A what?" He asked pulling back to look into her eyes.

"A memory moment. My Dad use to say that when something happened that was special. I want this visit to be special for you, too, Trace. Come on, you'll get chilled with no coat and coffee should be ready by now. Dawn's not far off and we'll have to get ready to get my truck. Jake Moss will probably be out with his snow plow early and I want to call him before he gets started." Trace followed her into the kitchen. "You pour the coffee. Scrambled eggs and sausage sound good to you?" She hung her coat on a hook inside the door and opened the fridge.

The phone rang. Lee turned. "Who in the world is calling at this hour?" She reached for the phone as she set the eggs and milk on the counter. "Hello?............Mom! What's wrong?......No. No. I'm Fine....Mom....there's no need to worry....I....I'm not alone, Mom." Lee leaned back against the counter and turned to look at Trace, reaching to take the cup of coffee he was holding out to her. "Trace is here."

"Is that who I think it is, Lee?"

"Yes, Mom, it is."

"Is everything all right?"

"Yes, Mom, everything is fine."

"Is he staying? Is he…?"

"We're talking about that. He's staying for Christmas, so I won't be alone for the holidays."

"Do you want me to come home?"

"No, Mom, there's no need for that! The storm is over. We just have to wait for the plows to clear the road so we can get into town to finish Christmas shopping. We need this time, Mom, to sort things out."

"OK, Lee. I trust your judgment even if your hormones are all out of balance at this moment. You've always had a good head on your shoulders and I know that you'll be fine. I do hope, dear, that you two are able to work things out. If you want to talk, you know how to get a hold of me."

"Yes, Mom. Thank you. Call me Christmas Eve, OK?"

"Bye Sweetheart. I'll talk to you then."

"I love you, Mom."

Trace was folding eggs and milk into a bowl as Lee hung up and reached to turn sausages in the pan. She glanced up at him. "That was Mom."

"I gathered. She knows about me?"

"Not really. I didn't tell her anything about you - not even your name. I just told her that I met a man and I wasn't careful."

Trace poured the egg mixture into the pan, set the bowl aside and turned to place his hands on Lee's shoulders. "I'm sorry, Lee. I didn't realize. I didn't know. I didn't mean to make things hard on you and you've had to face a lot alone. It can't have been easy. I don't know how to undo any of that or even how to make it up to you."

"Trace. I can't place all the blame on you. I made decisions from the very beginning that I have to take responsibility for. We've already talked about that. I never wanted anyone to think badly of you. I never mentioned your name to anyone. I never named you in any of this. In reality I didn't want anyone to think badly of me either. I thought silence was the best story of all. I thought about all of that last night. I thought about last summer…and…us…and…what happened…………"

Trace tucked his hand under her chin and lifted her face. "And what did you decide? Do you regret it? Have you changed your mind? Do you want me to go away?" His eyes searched her face, her eyes.

Slowly she shook her head. "No. No regrets. I never had any of those, Trace. I wanted what happened. I wanted to know you in that way. I wouldn't change any of it. I want a chance to feel it again. I want to give us a chance to sort this out. To see what we have….I don't want to lose you, Trace. I don't want to take that chance." She leaned forward, pressing her face against his chest as his fingers closed over her hair and his lips touched the top of her head. Burning hunger flamed inside of him as he breathed in her essence, his arms tightened, pulling her closer. She tilted her face up; his lips brushed her forehead, her eyes; her cheek and found her lips. They opened to his hungry mouth and he felt the same response in her he had before. For one brief moment he lost himself in that response then, shaking, he pulled away.

"God! Lee! I want you, but I won't hurt you. I'm afraid to hurt you."

There was a moment when she felt rejected before she realized that he was referring to her condition. She smiled and reached up to touch his lips with her fingertips. "I don't think it will hurt any of us. It's perfectly safe to share tenderness, love and giving." Her fingers trailed to the corner of his mouth, along his strong jaw, down his neck to the collar and slowly she began releasing the buttons of the warm blue plaid wool shirt. He took a deep breath and she felt his body trembling as her fingers brushed his skin, pulling aside the material. She leaned forward and trailed her lips where her fingers had burned across his chest.

"Lee!" His voice was low and husky. He lowered his head, breathing in the scent of her, his lips brushing the top of her head. He captured her hands in his and held them before his chest as his eyes searched hers.

"Tonight…...Can I lie beside you? Hold you? All night?"

"Yesss…Trace…..I want you to."

"I want to be with you. I want to spend this whole day starting over. But first we have to feed you two and get your truck." He turned back to the stove to stir the eggs.

After breakfast, Trace began washing dishes while Lee went to the phone.

"Hi, Louise. I hope it's not too early. How did you weather the storm?" A pause and then again her voice. "My truck is in the lane. Let me know when Jake's ready to go out and I'll meet him out there. Yes. Yes. I'm fine. A friend found me and brought me home." She hung up. "Be about an hour. Jake's been out on his snowmobile checking the road and stock. He's plowing their drive right now."

"Good." Trace replied as he rinsed the frying pan. He reached for a towel to dry his hands. "By the time I get the snow off my truck and get it warmed, we'll be ready to go. I'll go get ready."

An hour later, Louise called to say that Jake had just left the house. Lee dressed warmly and joined Trace. The truck eased slowly out of the yard and out to the road through wind packed snow drifts. Jake had already arrived at Lee's truck. Trace stopped, took Lee's keys and walked over to Jake who was sweeping snow off the stranded truck.

"Jake? Trace Little Horn. I'm a friend of Lee's."

"You the one found her out here last night?"

"Yeah."

"Good thing you came along. Not much traffic on this road except the people who live out here and not many of them out here after that storm hit. You want to start it? I'll finish getting this snow off."

Half an hour later, Lee's truck was back on the road. Trace followed her home. It had stopped snowing and the clouds had lifted some. Small patches of pale blue sky were visible.

"We better take advantage of the break in the weather." Lee said as she slipped in beside Trace.

Christmas lights, lengths of boughs and wreaths decorated the streets of town. People like themselves had taken advantage of the break and come out to do last minute shopping. Plows had cleared the main streets and parking lots.

"Where to first?" Trace asked. "You know the stores better than I."

"There's a couple of big stores at the shopping center. We should find everything we need or want there. Do you want to meet at the coffee shop when you're finished? Or do you want to meet me at the café by the grocery store?"

"Coffee shop sounds great. Give me a couple of hours?"

Trace watched as Lee walked away. He turned back to survey the selection of stores and shops – a book store, music shop, a jewelry store, a shoe store, a couple of clothing stores and gift shops. A sense of anticipation and excitement had begun to grow inside of him as he had listened to Lee's excited voice on the way in as she discussed some items she wanted to get for her mother. Voices raised in joyous carols drifted across the parking lot and more filled the wide hall of the shopping center as he stepped through the double doors. A huge decorated tree dominated the center of the hall. Beneath the tree two motorized reindeer dipped their heads in gentle movement. Just to the right of it, Santa sat upon wide steps that led up to a white sleigh overflowing with colorfully wrapped packages. A line of children waited to sit upon his lap. Trace stopped to watch as a young mother gently urged a small hesitant boy forward to the waiting arms of the smiling soft spoken Santa. A photographer was busy making notes while conversing with the mother of the child who had just been lifted down from Santa's lap.

Two hours later, Trace glanced at his watch. He was late. He tucked the last purchase inside a larger bag and hurried past the crowd still gathered around Santa. Outside in the last light of day, snow had begun to fall again. Trace turned toward the grocery store and the small coffee shop. The shop was crowded but Trace found Lee at a table in the back, a pile of packages at her feet and on the table.

"I'm sorry I'm late." Trace said as he moved a package and sat down across from her. "The place is crawling with people out shopping!"

Lee laughed as she looked at him. "They must have beaten you out. Do you want coffee?"

"Lee! How are you? How's your Mother?"

Trace turned as Lee looked up. The man in uniform had stepped closer, his gaze taking in the packages and Trace.

"Marc Walker! It's been a long time! I'm fine. And so is Mom. She's still visiting relatives out of state."

"You alone for the holidays?" The officer asked once again glancing at Trace.

"No. No. I have company from out of town. Officer Walker, this is my friend, Trace Little Horn from Seattle. He's an airline pilot." Walker did not extend his hand and Trace merely nodded as Lee went on. "Trace, meet Marcus Walker, one of our local sheriff's deputies. Marc and I went to school together."

"Horn? Sounds familiar. You from around here?"

Before Trace could answer, another officer appeared with two steaming cups of coffee. "OK Walker. I got the coffee. You get the donuts? We got to get back on the road. Sorry...Oh...Hi...didn't really pay attention enough to see you, Lee. I gotta keep an eye on this guy...always wandering off. You have a happy holiday...and be safe."

Walker turned to take the cup of coffee and the two officers, with a hasty farewell, worked their way back through the crowd.

Trace reached out to cover Lee's hand. "I'll get the coffee, you sit still. Just tell me what you want. And while I'm gone you can find the grocery list because that's our last stop. I don't want you too tired."

When he returned, he found her adding notes to the shopping list. He laughed. "Did I forget something?"

"Dinner tonight."

"Nope. I got that list all figured out...I'm cooking tonight...basic...but filling and good for you."

"Oh really? Dare I ask what?"

"Of course! Burgers and fries."

"Trace! You can't be serious?"

"What? Think I can't make a basic burger?"

Lee laughed at his hurt expression. "Wouldn't you rather have tacos with rice and refried beans? It's easy and won't take long to fix."

"When we get home, I want you to relax. I'm sure by the look of those packages that you have some wrapping to do. So I'll let you get all the supplies we need to do that while I make a mess of the kitchen. You don't mind do you?"

"No, I suppose not. As long as I don't have to spend half the night cleaning up after you!"

# CHAPTER 15

Snowflakes drifted lazily down from the darkened sky, glistening as they passed through the light shed by the lamp on the back porch and the lamp high on the post near the garage. The silence of the night broken only by the soft shushing of the snow as it fell and the sound of Christmas music from inside the open kitchen door.

Trace kicked snow from his boots as he crossed the porch to the door, packages tucked in both arms. He slipped his fingers around the screen door handle, tugged until it opened and wedged one foot in to pull it open enough to use his shoulder to hold it while he turned his body aside to gain entrance. The aroma of baking potatoes and fresh coffee filled the kitchen and he glanced at the stove where a pan of water boiled with four ears of corn.

The soft glow of colored lights from the Christmas tree was the only light in the living room. From upstairs came the rattle of paper and Lee's voice joining the Christmas carols playing on the stereo in her room. He smiled as he pushed open the door to the guest room and dropped his packages on the bed, then hurried back outside.

He had moved the grill from the back porch to the snow at the foot of the steps. Red coals winked at the bottom of the grill. Satisfied that they were ready, he returned to the kitchen, picked up a hot pad, opened the oven door and reached in to check the baking potatoes. He closed the oven door and tipped the lid over the pan of boiling water. From the fridge, he took a package of salmon, removed the plastic cover and returned to the grill.

Fifteen minutes later, steaming baked potatoes, ears of corn and grilled salmon were on platters on the table. Trace stopped at the foot of the stairs.

"Lee? Dinner's ready."

"Down in a minute." She replied.

By the time she appeared, Trace had poured coffee. He pulled a chair back for her and leaned to brush his lips along her cheek as she slid onto it.

"Mmmmmm. Smells delicious and looks great."

Trace offered the platter of salmon first, sliding the meat onto her plate as she scooped up a baked potato. "Butter or sour cream?" He asked as he slid into the chair opposite her. "I got fresh chives just for this."

"Butter for the corn. Sour cream for the potato." Lee answered. "And cream for my coffee?"

Trace chuckled. "I went fancy. I found that creamer on a shelf." He indicated the tiny eggshell blue colored pitcher next to the plain white porcelain sugar bowl.

"Oh. I didn't see that! I haven't seen it in some time actually. It was one of the few things my father brought home from his mountain treks and we never used it. He found it in a small wooden box buried near the rendezvous site. It was wrapped in oil cloth and packed in moss. There was also a silver sugar bowl and a small china teapot with brilliant blue lotus flowers edged in gold. Those are around here somewhere. I had completely forgotten about them."

"I hope you don't mind my using it then." Trace said softly.

"Oh, no! Not at all. How could you know? And… somehow… it seems… appropriate… a gift from my father…"

"Speaking of gifts…did you get all of yours wrapped?"

"Mmm…no……this salmon is great!! I think I'll keep you around!"

"Just for my salmon?" He laughed.

She shook her head as she took another bite of salmon. "Mmmm….no. Actually I kind of like looking at you. You know….something nice to look at across the table. But your cooking skills could carry some weight in the final decision."

Trace insisted that Lee sit at the table and only keep him company while he did the dishes and cleaned up the kitchen. They talked about her job, her mother, her father and the day of shopping just finished. At last, Trace wiped his hands dry, hung the towel and walked to the table where he reached for Lee's hands and pulled her to her feet. She stood before him, lifting her face, her eyes gazing up into his. She felt the warmth of his hands, the electric shock that his touch sent through her body, the trembling that began in the depth of her belly. The baby moved and quickly she guided his hand to the spot. He felt the movement, and looked down to watch as the fabric of her shirt moved with the ripple beneath his hand. As she watched his face she saw the glimmer of moisture that welled in his eyes. She saw the love that she had missed so many times and her breath caught in her throat.

"Oh, Trace." She said softly.

He lowered his head and touched her hair with his lips, his breath warm on her skin. He slipped his arms around her and pulled her close, holding her body against his gently and tenderly. His chin rested on the top of her head, her face tucked against his chest. "Come on." He said huskily as he released her. "We have some packages to finish wrapping."

The tree lights filled the living room with a soft glow that reflected from frosted window panes and glossy paper wrapped gifts beneath the lowest branches. Lee picked up several from the end of the couch and handed them to Trace. He knelt down to move packages and make room for more. Lee turned on some Christmas music and hurried upstairs to bring down more. "When are you going to wrap yours?" She asked as he set the last one in place. "I want to take a relaxing bath later. Why don't you wrap while I do that? I brought down a couple of photo albums I wanted you to see. They're on the coffee table, if you care to join me."

Trace joined her on the sofa as she opened the first album and soon she was sharing photos of her mother and father. Andrew McDougal had been a tall, well-built man, looking more like a rough woodsman than the wizened teacher of history that

Trace had pictured him to be. Lettie was also not as he had imagined. Somehow he had pictured her as a small frail older woman, but the woman who looked out at him from the photos was far from small and frail. While Lee bore a strong resemblance to both of her parents, she mirrored neither of them.

"Where did you get your red hair?" Trace asked as he scanned the photos.

Lee laughed. "My grandfather McDougal had great dark red hair my Dad said. And my eyes, he said were like my grandmother's. Dad's hair was the color of chestnuts and his eyes were hazel. Mom is blonde with blue eyes – she was really beautiful when she was younger."

"She didn't lose her looks with years." Trace commented.

"No. She didn't." Lee agreed. "But it changed. She became more sophisticated and yet softer in a gentle mature way. I guess that comes from the old south. Her family traces its roots back to the antebellum south. Her maiden name was Grant, said to be related to Ulysses S. Grant, but I don't know if that's true or just a family story. She was born in Savannah, Georgia. Her mother was from Louisiana where her family had lived for several generations. Southern plantations, cotton, rice and fine horses. Mother grew up on what was left of an old plantation on the outskirts of Savannah. She went to one of the best finishing schools the old south left to offer girls from families that could afford it. She went to Georgia State and graduated with a degree and intended to teach the fine art of grace, femininity, etiquette and more in her own studio. But before she could get started, her best friend suggested that she attend some business classes at Virginia State. So mother packed up and went back to school. That was where she met my father. He was teaching at a local school and taking undergrad studies at Virginia State. Mother didn't want to give up her idea of private training for young girls so after the first year she literally ran away from him and went home. It took him a year to find her and another to convince her to marry him and move to Kentucky where he had just landed a summer archeology position. For the next ten years, they traveled up and down the eastern states chasing teaching positions and summer archeology projects. I was unexpected, after four miscarriages. I was born in Nashville, Tennessee. When I was five, Dad accepted a position teaching history here and loved it, so we stayed."

"Lee, you don't talk about it...but...what happened to your father?"

There was a moment of silence as Lee picked up a photo of her father – one she had taken. Sun bronzed, dressed in a light tan tank top shirt and blue jeans holding up a rusted gold pan in one hand and a broken pick axe in the other as he leaned against a huge outcropping of solid bedrock. Lee smiled as she handed the photo to Trace. "We don't really know." She said softly. And told him the story of that summer. When she finished, neither spoke for a moment. Trace broke the quiet that had fallen between them.

"Do you think he went to the old mines?"

"I'm not sure. I don't know why he would. But we searched them and found no indication that he had been there." She was quiet again for a moment. "Trace?"

"Yes?"

"Do you think there really are caves up there?"

"I suppose it is possible. My grandfather said there were. Maybe your Dad found one."

Lee placed the last of the photos back into the box, set it aside and leaned back, closing her eyes. Trace had turned his attention to the tree, watching the lights wink off and on, noted the colors reflecting off the designs that frost had painted on the edge of the windows. He turned back to Lee, and, seeing her eyes closed, leaned back himself to study her.

Her hair was longer than it had been last summer, falling softly upon her shoulders. The winking colored lights played across the smooth skin of her face adding to the soft healthy glow that graced women who were with child. As he studied her features, he began to see a bit of each parent. He leaned toward her, brushing her cheek with his lips. She smiled as his lips traced a path to her lips, lingering as his breath caressed them. She reached up to touch his cheek.

"Come on sleepy head," He whispered, "don't you think it's time to turn in?"

She opened her eyes, still smiling, her fingers moved gently across his face, reaching up into his hairline. "Not until you kiss me." She whispered back as her fingers slid to the back of his head pressing his lips against hers. She tasted the

173

intoxicating essence of his lips and opened hers to allow him to take the kiss deeper as his hand framed her chin and warmth spread quickly through her body, igniting a fire that teased the inner depths of her being with sensations that began to flow along every nerve of her body.

Trace felt her response and his breath quickened, his own body responding. Her tongue teased his and he felt as if he were falling into a bottomless pit. He pulled away shaking and stood up, reaching for her hands to pull her up. She stood and moved toward the stairs, pausing at the bottom step and turning. Trace turned off the tree lights and moved across the room to join her. For one moment he stood looking up at her. Neither of them spoke, she lifted her hand and he took it in his and slowly mounted the stairs behind her.

There was a bed side lamp on in her room. She did not release Trace's hand until she stopped at the side of the bed and reached out to pull back the covers. Then she turned back, slipping her arms around him, tucking her hands beneath the hem of his shirt and slid them around beneath his arms and up his chest until her fingertips touched the hard nipples on his chest. He sucked in his breath, looking deeply into her eyes as he lifted his hand to her shoulders, then up to tangle them in the lengths of her hair as he lowered his head until his lips touched hers. Her mouth opened to accept his and for one moment they stood quiet allowing the sensations to well from deep inside and flow through them as they had never done before. Lee was acutely aware of

Trace and allowed herself to relax in his grip as the force of their shared emotions flowed between them.

Trace broke away, stepping back and still holding her gaze, he lowered his hands to loosen the buttons of her smock. His fingers touched her skin and she trembled. When he lifted the hem to pull the smock upward, she lifted her arms. Slowly, deliberately, Trace removed her clothes. When she stood before him, naked, he sat down on the bed and laid his open palms against her swollen belly. The taut skin of her belly rippled as the baby moved and he placed his hands over the rippling movement. He pulled her down to the bed and as she stretched out, he stood and began to remove his shirt and jeans. He sat back down and turned once more, his eyes taking in every inch of her body. From the red hair on the pale yellow pillowcase, to brilliant emerald green eyes, to breasts and hard, dark nipples enlarged by pregnancy, across the mound that was the child they had made, and down to her long legs. He leaned toward her and allowed his tongue to play against a dark nipple. He heard the indrawn breath, felt the tremor passing through her body. He stretched out beside her, pulling her against him.

"I want to hold you all night. Feel your body against mine. Breathe in your scent. I just want to feel you, smell you, taste you."

"Trace," Lee whispered "I've thought of this so often, I ached with the wanting. I can't believe we're here together….like this."

Trace kissed the top of her head and murmured. "Me too. Are you warm enough?" He pulled the covers up and tucked them around her, then slipped his arms around her once more. She pillowed her head against his shoulder and sighed contentedly.

\*\*\*\*\*

Lee moved and Trace woke. "What's wrong?"

"Nothing," She said softly "but I have to get up. Keep this spot warm, I'll be right back."

A few minutes later when she slipped back into bed, she snuggled against Trace's back and trailed her lips against his skin. He rolled over wrapping his arms around her and her lips found his nipples as her hand slid below his waist.

"No, Lee." He said softly.

"Yes." She replied and closed her hand around him, feeling the response. He groaned softly and reached down to grasp her hips to pull her closer.

"No. Let me do this." She pushed his hand away.

"Oh, Lee. No."

"Yes." She whispered as she closed her lips over his nipple and held his hardness, working it with her fingers. She lifted up, shifting her weight, released his nipple and trailed her tongue down his ribs to his belly and then began a trail of kisses to his lower left abdomen just in the tuck of his hip.

"Lee!" His voice was ragged and hoarse and she felt the tension ripple through his body. His fingers curled in her hair, his head lifted from the pillow, he gasped and shuddered as her manipulation brought his release.

Lee moved to close her lips over his, then slipped off the bed. When she returned she turned on the lamp, and laid a warm wash cloth on Trace's belly. He opened his eyes and looked up at her. "Lee. I'm sorry…"

She smiled and sat down to reach out and take the cloth and began washing his belly. "No need for that. I wanted to make love to you."

"You surprise me." He said softly.

"Why?"

"I don't know. I guess I didn't expect you to… you know…"

"I'm not totally naïve… I may not be as experienced as you… but somehow touching you… even with how things have been between us… everything seems so…natural… so… easy…I wanted to touch you…I wanted to love you…and nothing touches me so deeply as seeing and feeling your response…your love…more deeply than I could have imagined…"

"Lee…Don't think for one moment that I have lots of experience. This… what just happened… Lee… you're so wonderful…you're such a loving and giving woman…you know how to touch on a deep level… you keep opening up new insights to the depth of yourself. I see a new you with every experience…with every hour we spend together. And I think I fall a little deeper in love with you every time."

\*\*\*\*\*

Movement woke Trace, an odd sensation against his back. Then he smiled as he realized that Lee lay against him, her belly touching his back and the movement of the baby had awakened him. He didn't want to move or speak for fear of disturbing either, so he remained unmoving and still; absorbing the sensations of his child and the woman he knew he loved. He listened to the slow even breathing, felt her breath against his back.

Lee murmured softly in her sleep and readjusted her body, slipping an arm over Trace's ribs as she snuggled closer. The baby rolled and kicked and Trace felt the strength of the child as it moved in the confined space. "Mine." He thought as emotions tumbled inside him as the baby tumbled inside of Lee. For the first time in his life he felt an attachment to someone – different than that he felt for Lee. This life was so helpless, so dependent upon Lee and even himself. This was a life that could be shaped, guided in the same manner as his grandfather had done with him when he was small. For the first time in many years he wished that he could see and hear his own father; wished that he could feel his father's love and wondered if it had been close to what he was feeling for this unborn child. But even as these thoughts came, he felt the familiar comfort of his grandfather and knew that his father would have felt the same to him.

Lee rolled away and Trace slipped out of bed, stopping momentarily to assure that his movements had not awakened her. He moved across the room to the window and looked out upon the yard below. Snow still fell lazily from the darkened sky. 'Peace." He thought. "Peace and love. This is what it feels like. Soft and gentle and pure as a new snow flake. Changing the world around you without grinding force. Making the world seem so much bigger, so much brighter and purer. It's as if life suddenly extended into forever."

"The meaning of life, my son." Trace whirled around at the quiet voice. Lee moved in her sleep. Through the open doorway, soft light lay across the floor. Trace glanced at the bed, then moved toward the open doorway. He was sure it was his grandfather's voice he had heard and he was also sure that there were no lights on that could cast that soft glow of light upon the hallway floor. When he reached the hallway, the light was upon the stairs and he followed. Trace stopped on the bottom step, the tree lights winked in the pre-dawn darkness in the living room. Lights he was sure he had turned off.

"The greatest gift we can give is love." The voice came from the direction of the tree and yet flowed from all over the room. A soft halo of light surrounded the angel atop the tree.

"Grandfather?" Trace whispered. The room was silent. The light from the tree softened and faded until the only light was that reflected from beyond the windows. The light from the big yard light and the lightening of the sky as daylight pushed forward.

Trace padded soundlessly to the kitchen to make coffee. When it was done, he poured a cup and went to the room he had slept in alone. He turned on the light, closed the door and approached the pile of shopping bags on the bed. Lee had placed wrapping paper, ribbon, bows and tape on top and he set those aside to begin opening the bags. Carefully he boxed, wrapped, taped and ribboned. When he was finished he took the packages out to arrange them under the tree mixing them up with packages Lee had already placed there. One last package, he tucked into the corner of the top dresser drawer. With a fresh cup of coffee in hand, he stood at the door, his gaze lingering on the tree. Had he imagined the earlier events? Had he gotten up still caught in the last stages of sleep thinking he was wide awake and alert when in fact he had been in half dream state? Hours of flying, driving and concern for Lee had surely played a part in what had happened. Trace shook his head and sipped coffee.

"Trace? Is everything all right?"

Trace looked up. Lee stood at the top of the stairs looking half asleep herself.

"I couldn't sleep. Ready for a cup? Or are you not up yet?"

"Mmmm... not really awake... but... I missed you... and a cup would wake me up. Would you mind awful much?"

"Not at all. Ready for a bite to eat or do you want to wait and wake up fully first?"

"Toast and jam. Coffee. I'll be right down. Let me wash the sleep out of my eyes and off my face."

"You got it." But she had already disappeared. When she came downstairs, the plate and cup were on the coffee table and Trace was waiting. Lee settled into the corner of the couch as Trace held out the plate of toast.

"Got any plans for today?" Trace asked as she sipped coffee and ate her toast. "Tomorrow's Christmas Eve."

"Are you finished shopping?" She asked.

"Mmmhhmm… wrapped this morning. Everything under the tree and waiting only for the arrival of Santa."

"I thought I'd spend the day baking."

"Baking? What?"

"Christmas cookies. There are tins of homemade peanut brittle, fudge, divinity, mints and fruit cake in the pantry. I've been getting ready since Thanksgiving, but I thought most of it would wait until mom got home. I'll make sugar cookies, ginger snaps and molasses cookies. Tomorrow morning I'll make bread dough and pie dough and start the stuffing mix. We'll have fresh twists and croissants; put together a couple of baskets of goodies to take to Christmas Eve mass. When we get home, I'll stuff the turkey and set it on slow bake ready for Christmas dinner."

"I was thinking… I'm only here for a few more days… and I didn't see a crib…can we pick one up tomorrow morning? I want to help you get ready… make sure you have everything you need."

"Well…I do sort of have one…mine….mom and dad carted it around and it's in the loft above the garage… or at least it was the last time I recall seeing it. If you want to go look we can do that after I get dressed."

*****

"I haven't been up here in a couple of years." Lee said as she pushed open the door at the top of the narrow stairs. The attic room was cool, but not uncomfortably so. Two light bulbs cast a warm glow in the long narrow room where dust covered sheets draped mystery piles.

Lee tugged a sheet and revealed three old steamer trunks piled one on top the other. The bottom one was metal; the second two were metal and wood – all with large round brass clasps and leather straps. She replaced the sheet and moved on. The next two piles were old wooden packing crates. The third pile was also wooden packing crates with open tops revealing old text books. There was a table with woven baskets and old dried flowers under one sheet. An old rocker with a broken arm, two kitchen chairs with broken reed seats, two narrow cherry wood bookcases, an old tricycle, a red wagon with no rear wheel; a large crock on a small homemade bench, a swag lamp with torn fringe, a pole lamp with Tiffany shade and worn cord. There were more wooden packing crates, some cardboard boxes and then an old trundle bed.

Lee brushed her dusty hands on her slacks and looked up and down the room. "Wow. I had forgotten half this stuff. That Tiffany lamp was my grandmother's. The wagon was mine – Dad and I took the wheels off to put on a set of runners he made one winter. I bet the books were their college books. The only place we haven't looked is that clutter behind the stair."

The clutter turned out to be two old iron bedsteads with wire springs. Behind these they found the crib. It wasn't as big as Lee remembered and it was in pieces. Trace laid it out to make sure that everything was still there. "I think it needs a bit of work." He said as he inspected the rollers and bars. "Is there a shop in town that can do it?"

"In Sand Point."

"I'll drop it off."

Trace carried the pieces down stairs ready to load into his truck when he left after Christmas. By the time he finished, Lee had washed up, poured more coffee and was already mixing cookie dough.

By late afternoon, the house was filled with the aroma of fresh baked cookies and bread. Trays of cookies cooled on the counter - molasses, sugar cookies in the shape of candy canes and trees, ginger snaps, oatmeal and chocolate chip. Brownies, fudge and divinity were on the counter ready to go into waxed boxes or paper to be boxed. Cinnamon rolls and cinnamon twists cooled beside them with racks of fluffy croissants and mincemeat and jelly tarts.

Trace helped clean up the last of the baking dishes and then began laying out preparation for making diner while Lee went to shower and freshen up after a day of working in a hot kitchen. He had enjoyed spending the day, reading recipes, mixing ingredients, spooning out dough, pouring out batter, setting out cookies to cool and then cleaning up to start all over again. They had bantered, shared, talked and played at the holiday project. He wanted dinner to be perfect after a perfect day of togetherness. He mixed and rolled left over salmon with seasonings and made salmon patties, mashed potatoes with garlic and, soon, corn on the cob, fresh biscuits and salad were also set on the table for dinner.

Trace poured chilled sparkling cider into amber colored wine glasses, lit two red tapered candles in short slender silver holders in the center of the table and stepped back to turn off the overhead light. He looked up as Lee entered, fresh from a shower and dressed in a long green velvet skirt and ivory blouse that billowed softly over her swollen stomach. He paused, drinking in the scene.

"Lee." His voice just above a whisper. "You're... you're beautiful."

Lee smiled as she took in the kitchen scene and Trace. "Thank you, kind sir." She answered. "I wasn't quite expecting candles."

"Candles seemed to be the right touch, but they've enhanced everything soft about you. Makes you look like an angel." He moved around the table, placed his hands on her shoulders and lowered his face to kiss her lips and breathe in her sweetness. He stepped back. "Thank you for letting me stay, Lee... for giving me this chance. It's the best gift I've ever been given."

Lee looked up into his eyes and caught her breath at the reflection of deep love, the glimmer of tears. "You've made my Christmas very special, Trace. I love you." She reached up and placed her right hand on his cheek.

Trace covered her hand with his own, then moved it to his lips, kissing the open palm as he caressed her cheek with his fingers. "I love you, too, Lee. More than words can ever say."

The phone rang and Lee moved to answer it. "Hello?"

"Merry Christmas, honey." Her mother said.

"Merry Christmas, Mom. I didn't expect to hear from you until tomorrow."

"We've just come back from church and I wanted to speak to you before you left home. You are going to Christmas services? I wanted you to know that I miss you and I wish I were there."

"Oh, Mom! I miss you, too. But don't let that stop you from enjoying your family there."

"How are things going, dear? You know I'm concerned about all of this. How long is your young man staying?"

"The day after Christmas, Mom. Things are going great. We spent a day shopping. Today we did Christmas cooking and dug out my old crib. How are things there?"

"Oh my goodness! I had forgotten about your old crib! I'm glad you found it, but it probably needs some attention after all these years."

"Trace is going to take it to a shop in Sand Point to have it refinished. If we start now, it'll be ready by March. We'll talk more tomorrow, Mom, we were just sitting down to dinner. I love you and miss you."

Lee hung up and turned back into Trace's arms. He pulled her against him, pressing her head into his chest as he placed his cheek against the top of her head. "I love you, Lee. I am more sure of that every day."

"Stop it before you make me sappy! Sit down and serve up dinner. We still have work to do."

After dinner, they shared the cleanup and dish washing. When everything was put away, Lee went to the pantry to bring out wax paper, Christmas tins and boxes. Trace lined up platters of cookies, candy and breads and together they began putting together gift boxes. After each one was filled, Lee selected a colorful ribbon and bow and finished the gift with a name tag. When they finished, there were more dishes to do before the boxes went into bags and boxes by the door.

"It's an old family tradition." Lee smiled as she set the last one down. "I still have a few packages to wrap before bed. Are you done?"

"Me? Done? I haven't even started! Need some help?"

"Nope! And you are on your own!" She headed upstairs as Trace turned off kitchen lights and retreated to the quiet of his room. As he wrapped the last of the gifts, Trace became more and more aware of the warmth and comforting feeling of family, something he suddenly realized that he had felt fleetingly in the few years spent with his grandfather, aunt and uncle. While then he had always felt like something was missing, this felt right. It filled his heart as nothing had since his childhood. As he opened the dark blue velvet box and looked at the simple diamond nestled within, he wondered if he was doing the right thing. Would Lee accept? If she did, they would have many things to discuss before he left. He set the box on the nightstand, picked up a pile of presents and toed the door open. There was silence upstairs as Trace arranged gifts under the tree. He moved to the stairs and hesitated on the bottom step, then taking a deep breath he climbed slowly, listening. The upper hall was dark except for the sliver of light beneath Lee's door. Trace stopped, then tapped gently.

"It's open." Lee called out, but the door opened before he could turn the knob. "You're just in time. I'll take these and you can get those off the bed." She swept past him holding up red velvet stockings with candy canes draped over the tops. Trace picked up an arm full of packages and followed. Lee stepped back from the tree where she had set the stockings and watched as Trace set his burden down and stepped back.

"Looks as if Santa has already been here." He remarked as he slipped an arm around Lee's shoulder.

She smiled up at him. "It feels right for the first time in years."

He hugged her to him as he kissed the top of her head. "I feel the same way, Lee. I hope we can share many of these."

Lee pulled away, taking his hand. "Come on, I'm beat. We had a full day and tomorrow we have lots to do. We'll need an early start."

Trace let her lead him upstairs again. He watched as she pulled the shirt over her head and began removing her slacks. He undressed and slid into bed beside her, slipping his arm around her shoulders and pulling her against him. She reached out to turn off the light and snuggled against him.

He lifted her face and kissed her warm lips. "Good night, Lee. I love you." He whispered.

"Mmmm me, too." She answered sleepily and he smiled as he realized how quickly she had relaxed against him, how quickly she was drifting off to sleep.

*****

"Wake up, sleepy head! We have lots to do and daylight's a wastin!" Trace opened his eyes. Lee stood by the bed, already dressed, a cup of coffee in both hands. "Biscuits, gravy and eggs and bacon are on the table."

"What time is it? How long have you been up and how did I sleep through all of this?"

Lee laughed as he sat up and took the coffee. "I slipped out of bed quietly a couple of hours ago. You were sleeping soundly."

Trace dressed quickly and followed Lee downstairs. After breakfast, they cleaned up the kitchen and Trace went to warm his truck while Lee began preparing boxes and baskets for him to carry out. Trace laughed as the last one was packed in. "I feel a little like Santa Claus with all this stuffed in here ready for delivery!"

A good part of the day was spent knocking on doors, handing out boxes and baskets and exchanging holiday greetings. By midafternoon, they were home; ham and potatoes were baking and they were putting away the contents of boxes and baskets they had collected as they delivered. Three wrapped hams and several packages of beef and elk were put into the freezer along with bags of frozen green beans and corn from last year's local gardens. Jars of jellies, jams and preserves were stacked onto pantry shelves. Fresh new home made dish cloths, oven pads and dish towels were folded and put away.

The last of the baskets and boxes to be delivered were packed into the truck to be unloaded at church. The church was already crowded when they arrived, but Lee managed to find and exchange greetings with those who would receive gifts after the service. Trace did not feel like a stranger as he mingled with people Lee had known all of her life. Everyone asked after her mother and offered greetings to be forwarded at the first opportunity. They found seats and exchanged more greetings. During the service, Lee slipped her hand into Trace's and he released it only to light her candle at the end. As the people poured solemnly out of the chapel, some separated to speak to them. Trace left Lee to go get the packages and they talked as friends gathered to exchange gifts. When at last they stepped out into the cold crisp night air, Lee tucked her hand beneath Trace's arm, while he carried packages to the truck.

By the time they pulled into the driveway, Lee's head rested lightly on Trace's shoulder. He shifted to wake her and sleepily she allowed him to guide her into the house and upstairs to bed. After she was tucked in, Trace went back out to bring in the packages from church and then turned out the lights and slipped into bed beside her.

*****

"Trace. Trace." The voice penetrated his sleep and slowly Trace lifted to its' call. He lay without moving; listening. Lee still lay snuggled against him, making small noises in her sleep. He felt the ripple of movement as the baby moved about. The light glow of moonlight softened the darkness in the room. Trace pushed the covers away and eased his body away from Lee's as he slipped from the bed. He turned to pull the covers back up and his eyes lingered on the sleeping form in bed. Her red hair laid out on the pillow, one hand tucked beneath a cheek. He reached out, placed his hand above her cheek then pulled back without touching her and turned toward the window.

Snow glistened as the light of the moon washed across the surface of the ground. Beneath the more brilliant light of the yard light at the gate, crystals of snow winked like tiny stars. As his gaze lifted to the trees and the towering mountain above, Trace almost expected to see a reindeer drawn sleigh move across the sky. Instead, he was drawn to study the dark looming mass of Ghost Cave Mountain, and for one brief moment, he thought he saw winking lights high up on the craggy lower peak. He studied the horizon and guessed that dawn wasn't far off and slowly turned back into the room. Picking up his shirt and shorts, he stepped into the hallway, closing the door softly behind him. Some quick rearrangements downstairs and one stocking bulged more than it had the night before. The little velvet box now waited in the toe of Lee's stocking. Satisfied, Trace turned on the tree lights and went into the kitchen to make coffee.

With a mug of hot coffee in hand, Trace settled onto the couch, watching the twinkling lights play sparkling patterns across foil wrapped packages beneath the tree. His thoughts slipped back to childhood Christmas mornings when the tree had been a small one his grandfather had brought in, the decorations handmade – strings of colored paper coils, colored popcorn, dried cranberries and corn. He could hear the Christmas music coming from the square brown wood radio his grandfather had treasured, his aunt humming softly. He could see his cousins seated on the floor around the table where the tree stood, waiting expectantly for the gifts to be handed round. Lost in these thoughts, he didn't hear Lee and was startled as she reached out to touch his shoulder, a cup of steaming coffee in her other hand.

"Where were you?" She smiled.

"Yesteryear." He replied as he pulled her down beside him. She snuggled against him for a moment before sitting up as the phone rang. "Your mother." He laughed. "I'll get it."

"Merry Christmas, Mom." Lee sang into the phone.

"Merry Christmas, darling. I suppose I called too early?"

"If you mean that we haven't opened gifts, the answer is yes. If you mean did you get us up, the answer is no. How is your Christmas going?"

"The house is already filling up with relatives. We opened gifts a couple of hours ago, but the day doesn't feel right without starting it by talking to you."

"I miss you, too, Mom, but I'm glad you are with family you haven't spent holidays with in years. It stopped snowing during the night; it's a beautiful day here. How about there?"

Her mother laughed. "No snow. Heavy clouds and a light rainfall this morning. Christmas without snow doesn't feel quite like Christmas. But I do remember quite a few just like this when I was growing up. Thank you for the lovely sweater, dear and the gifts cards."

"I did some extra shopping late. There will be a few things to open when you get back home. I'll call you back after we finish here, OK?"

"Yes. Bye, dear."

Lee handed the phone back to Trace, as he handed her the first gift to open.

An hour later, they sat on the couch surrounded by boxes and piles of paper. Lee ran her fingers over the soft fabric of a pale blue sweater her mother had sent and then picked up the white silk scarf Trace had given her. Her eyes swept over colored candles, warm gray mittens, a red woolen lap blanket, new shirts, a book about Native American Indian tribes, a lamb's wool steering wheel cover, a basket of canned meats and wrapped cheeses, gift soaps and perfumes.

"You're not done, yet." Trace said as he handed her the bulging stocking. She laughed as scooped out candies and nuts and then the half dozen small gifts – a small bottle of perfume, travel soaps, note pad and pens, gift certificates for a coffee shop, a book store, a local clothing store and a couple of fast food restaurants and then the blue velvet box. She held it for a moment without looking at Trace and almost afraid to open the box. She wasn't sure what she was expecting, but a tear slipped down her cheek as she opened it and saw the single sparkling diamond.

Trace watched her face, noted the tear, but was afraid to speak or move.

Lee moved slowly, lifting the ring from its' velvet cushion, she looked up and lifted the ring, reaching out to Trace. She saw the expression on his face, in his eyes and smiled through her own tears. "Don't you think you should slip it on?" She whispered.

Trace sank to the floor at her knees. "Does that mean what I think it does?"

"Does this mean what I think it does?" She returned with a timid smile.

"I hope so." He replied as he took the ring and her left hand. "I've been afraid to ask. I don't know if it's too early, too late or not soon enough. I don't know if it's the right time, but I know that deep inside it feels like the right thing to me. And I was hoping you felt the same way. I love you, Lee. I want to spend the rest of my life with you. I want to be there for you. I want to be there for our children…our family. I want you to be my family. And I want this baby to be the start of that family. Will you accept this ring and my love, Lee? Will you marry me? It doesn't have to be right away. I'm willing to wait until you're ready. I just need to know that you feel the same. Will you be my wife, my partner, my friend, my companion, my love?"

Tears streamed down Lee's cheeks as her fingers curled around his hand. "Trace, I love you. Get that ring on my finger before I cry too hard to hold still."

He held her hand, watching the diamond sparkle on her finger; he kissed her finger tips, turned her hand over and kissed the palm. He laid his head on her lap as she ran her fingers through his hair. He heard her sob, felt the rush of tears as he gathered her into his arms.

"I won't rush you. We have lots to talk about. There's time. You let me know when. I just hope it's soon. I love you, Lee and I want this to work out. This scares the hell out of me, but I want it and I want you in my life."

"Whatever happens, Trace, that is what this is all about. Standing side by side, working together to solve problems and make it all work out for the best – for everyone. I don't want to wait. I want to be married before the baby is born, but I want that to be our ceremony and I'd like another when Mom gets home. Do you think we can do that?"

"I'll take some time off. Would you like a Valentine wedding in Sand Point? And then you and your mother can plan the reaffirmation whenever you want. We'll have to bide time until I can either transfer closer or get another job. It may take a few months. I'll start checking when I get back to Seattle."

"We have a life time, Trace."

*****

Trace wadded up paper, packed torn ribbons and bows into a box and began breaking down other boxes and compacting them in with the paper and ribbons. From the kitchen came the aroma of spices as Lee mixed ingredients for stuffing. When Trace completed picking up, he turned to the sofa where he had placed his own pile of gifts: a black and white sweater, a book about Idaho history, midnight blue leather map pouch, water tight pouch for camera and another for maps, a small framed photo of Lee, an Idaho key chain and a pair of warm lined driving gloves. He picked them up and placed them beneath the tree with the red net bag containing nuts and oranges and the box of Christmas candies and baked goods.

The phone rang and he heard Lee answer. "Merry Christmas, Kevin!"

He stepped into the kitchen and she smiled at him, passed a bowl of damp, buttery, spiced warm bread crumbs and waved at the turkey waiting on the side board. As she talked to her boss, he scooped the contents of the bowl into the open cavity of the turkey.

"Thanks, Kevin, but I have dinner plans. I really appreciate you thinking of me." She hung up as Trace finished the stuffing and stepped back to let her finish the project, then picked up the pan as she opened the oven door. Together, they prepared their first Christmas dinner.

Karen J. Simon

# CHAPTER 16

Trace tucked the last of his clothes into his bag and set it on the floor. Lee sat on the edge of the bed watching. Her thoughts tumbled over the events of the past few days. The holiday had sped by so quickly, she suddenly realized. She wasn't ready to say good bye. Wasn't ready to face the empty days ahead – waiting. Trace turned to see the expression on her face and reached out to lift her chin gently.

"I'll call every day. I'll be back as soon as I can." He leaned forward and trailed kisses across her forehead.

A tear slipped down her cheek as she reached up to touch his face. "I've been so happy these past few days. It all happened so fast. I'm almost afraid I'll wake up and find it was just a dream."

"Then let's neither of us wake up." He said tenderly as he pulled her against him. "Let me finish packing the truck so that we can take advantage of these last few hours."

Lee pulled away, wiped the tears from her cheeks and smiled up at Trace. "Go. I'll fix some hot chocolate and meet you back here."

Lee went to the kitchen and began making up small sealed containers of leftovers to send with Trace. She put water on to boil, scooped powdered chocolate into cups and turned to the platter of turkey.

The kitchen door opened. "Lee, where did you get these?"

Lee turned as Trace placed an old coffee tin on the table.

"What is it?" She asked.

"I'm not sure what all is here, but this can fell of a shelf I bumped moving the crib pieces. The lid came off and this fell out." Lee held up an object that rattled as he moved it.

"What is it?" Lee asked again.

"A medicine rattle - made of two turtle shells laced together and filled with small pebbles."

Lee took the object and rolled it over in her hands, studying it. "I've never seen it before. But it must have been something my father found. I wonder why he never mentioned it, and why he brought it home. Is there more in there?" She indicated the can with a small hand movement.

Trace reached into the can and pulled out a piece of cloth that smelled of saddle soap. He turned it over and pulled the ends. Nestled in the cloth saturated with saddle soap was a leather bag, dark with age. Beneath the cloth was another carefully wrapped object that turned out to be a small pipe – in three pieces. As her fingers traced the pattern carved into the surface of the bone bowl, Lee wondered again at her father's silence regarding these discoveries.

"I think your father found a medicine cave."

"I never heard of them until you spoke of them." Lee said as she picked up the can to study it as if there might be some indication of where it and the items had come from. "He spent so much time over the years on that mountain. He never mentioned caves or medicine men. Surely he would have known about them?"

"Our people would never speak of these to white men and even if they did, they would never hint at location. So much time has passed since our people lived on the mountain, I'm not sure that anyone knows about them or their whereabouts."

"Your grandfather did and he spoke to you, so surely there could be others?"

"My grandfather called the stories legends. I don't know what he believed or knew. Legends are stories that add life and substance to traditions, history and just plain stories and sometimes they embellish the story so that you have to find the truth in it. Your father may have stumbled onto something that was used for ceremonies or ceremony preparation. And it may not be a cave. It may have been a rock over hanging, a niche in a stone wall, an abandoned animal den or the entrance of an old underground stream gone dry. This mountain has been walked and worked by people for so many years; it would seem that caves would have been discovered. But again it is possible that the entrance was well concealed by trees and brush and possibly became visible after a fire. The possibilities are many.

There may have been a reason for your father to remove the artifacts in order to preserve them.

"Do you know what these markings mean?" Lee asked turning the pieces in her hand.

"Not all of them. But sometimes pipes were created for specific purposes. The zig zag lines may indicate lightening, especially close to the clouds with rain drops falling. This may have been used for rain dances. The medicine men would not have shared the power they put into the pipe."

Lee picked up the aged leather bag, turning it over to look at the beads on the front. "Tobacco?"

"That I can't answer." Trace replied as he touched the beads. "Let's put them back, we'll finish cleaning them up and get a better look when I get back. In the meantime, put them into a better container and store them inside. I'll finish packing the truck."

It was close to noon when Trace had finished. Lee watched the hands move all too quickly around the face of the kitchen clock as she packed turkey sandwiches and plastic bowls of stuffing, cranberries, salad, candied yams, a thermos of fresh hot coffee and a box of cookies, fruit cake, biscuits, bread and candy.

The boxes of food were the last items packed into the front seat of Trace's truck. Lee stood on the back steps and watched as tears slipped down her cheeks. Trace closed the door and turned to mount the steps. He reached out to touch the tears and with his thumb softly brushed them away.

"Don't cry, Baby. It's only for a short time and I will be back. You can count on that. We'll talk often. You take care and keep me posted on all progress. OK?"

Lee was afraid to trust her voice. She pressed her cheek into Trace's hand and nodded as more tears flowed.

Trace pulled her into his arms, his hands caressed her hair as he kissed the top of her head. He tilted her chin up and his lips moved across her forehead, her cheeks and lingered on her tear damp lips.

"I don't know what's wrong with me." She whispered. "I'm afraid this has all been a dream. I'm afraid you won't come back. It all happened so fast. I'm afraid to let you go. I don't understand."

"Your emotions are heightened by your condition and all you've been through. I understand. I'm here for you. Just a phone call away. Remember that. And remember that I care very deeply for you. I want to be here. With you and our baby."

He stepped back. Lee reached out, touched the front of his jacket, reached up to touch his cheek.

"Come back." She whispered tearfully. She stood on the porch, watching as the truck disappeared down the drive and out to the lane. She took a deep shuddering breath and hurried into the warmth of the kitchen, closing the door and leaning her back against it as tears ran unchecked down her cheeks and sobs wracked her body. Her arms held close about her swollen belly, she rocked, feeling the sudden silence and loneliness that had settled over the house with Trace's departure. The phone rang. She brushed the tears away and grabbed it off the counter, swallowing the sobs and calming her voice.

"Hello?"

"Lee?"

Suddenly she laughed. "Did you forget something?"

"Yeah. You! I just wanted you to know that I miss you already"

"Funny. That makes me feel better! I miss you, too. Drive careful."

\*\*\*\*\*

Fog shrouded the city when Trace dropped down off Snoqualmie Pass and into the drizzling rain that was Seattle's claim to fame. It was late, lights reflected from the surface of rain wet streets. A light breeze lifted tendrils of fog and wrapped them about street lights making their light waver and fade. A car slid through a red light and disappeared behind a shield of fog. Trace braked lightly and turned to climb the hill toward his apartment. The city had been pleasant for the time he had lived here, but suddenly he wanted nothing more than to be driving away from it. He found his apartment to be as empty and silent as Lee had found her own home. He put away the food Lee had packed, tossed his bags onto the couch and reached for the phone.

Lee answered on the third ring, her voice heavy with sleep.

"I knew I'd wake you, Hon, but I wanted to let you know that I just got back into Seattle. It doesn't feel like home anymore. Nothing ever will without you there. How are you doing?"

"The place is like a tomb without you here, Trace. I don't know how I'll make it. I'm glad you called. I don't care how late it is."

"I'll call you tomorrow. Get some sleep. I love you." Trace hung up the phone, turned out the lights and slipped into bed, listening to the rain against the window, his thoughts suddenly turning to another rain storm.

"Everything's going to be OK, Grampa." He said softly.

*****

Lee rolled over, tucked the covers around her shoulders and tried to block out the wave of loneliness that washed over her. Since Trace had gone, she had walked through the rooms of the house feeling the silence, the emptiness, the aloneness in every corner as she had never felt it before. That first time she had felt abandoned, used, hurt and humiliated and angry at herself. Those emotions and the thoughts that went with them had masked the emptiness, the loneliness. Now, she knew that Trace felt the same as she did and his absence hurt in a different way. She had no doubts that he would be back, but she knew that it wouldn't be soon enough. Every day would be endless without his voice, his touch, his presence. Every night would be empty and lonely without his body against hers, his breath on her skin.

The baby moved restlessly and Lee rubbed where the movement rippled her swollen belly. "I know you must be feeling what I am and not understanding it, baby." She whispered. "But I miss your daddy terribly and I can't wait to see him, touch him, kiss him. I can't wait for us to be family together. I can't wait to see or hold you either. I know that you are a part of him and I know that you will be so like him in so many ways."

Moonlight momentarily flooded the room as clouds parted and moved in the heavens. The soft light seemed to fill the room with peace and serenity that brought a lightness to Lee's heart. She slept.

*****

"Heard you were looking for a transfer, Trace." Wayne said as he adjusted the controls for decent into Anchorage. "I thought you liked this run?"

Trace turned from the breathtaking view of the moon bathed, snow covered mountains and flowing glaciers that lined Alaska's coast. "I love this run. I love this country. But there have been some changes that take priority. I guess I haven't been great company on the past several runs, have I?"

"Let's say that you haven't exactly been talkative, or social. Like you're somewhere else. Everything go OK over the holiday. Boss said you had something urgent come up. I just assumed that whatever it was has sort of taken your attention. But I didn't realize that it had affected your life so hard. I hope everything is OK. You don't need to talk about it. It's your business. I'm not prying. I was just surprised that you wanted out of this since you requested it and the last time we talked I had the impression that this was where you wanted to be."

"It was, Wayne. And maybe at some depth, still is. But I met someone before I ever worked for this company and it fell apart before it started. I just couldn't get it out of my system, so I went back. We're getting married on Valentine's Day. It's not the right time for her to leave her job, or move, so I thought it would be easier for me to make that adjustment."

"Sounds like this is pretty serious, Trace. If there's anything I can do to help, let me know."

"I don't want to leave the company. But if I can't get a position nearer to Sand Point, I may have to. I'll miss working with you, Wayne."

The tower cleared them for landing at that moment, and both men turned their attention to the task at hand. Mountain peaks loomed below them and to the right as the aircraft banked to come in over Cook Inlet and drop down over Earthquake Park to the end of the runway. The lights of Anchorage glistened and sparkled in the darkness as they touched down. As the whine of the engines died away, Wayne turned to Trace. "See you inside. Dinner at the Crow's Nest?"

"You're on." Trace answered as he picked up the clip board and began going over the last of the paperwork.

"Decided to come back?" Cheryl quipped as she handed him a cup of steaming coffee when he entered Operations. "Hope you had a great holiday."

"I did, Cheryl. Thank you. How about you?"

She smiled. "I went home. Traditional Christmas. All the family. Lots of kids. Up late nights visiting. It was good to come back here and rest! But I thought I would see you before Christmas. I have a gift for you."

"Oh, Cheryl. You shouldn't have done that!"

She slipped behind the counter, opened a desk drawer and withdrew a package wrapped in silver paper. She placed it on the counter in front of Trace. "Oh, it's not much." She said shyly.

Trace laid aside his brief case and coffee cup and picked up the package. Tucked in cotton in the box was a small ivory plane.

"Cheryl. This is beautiful. But I can't accept it."

"Why not?" She asked. "It's a gift."

"Of course, he'll accept it." Wayne said as he stepped up beside Trace and reached out to take the box and examine the contents. "I haven't been able to educate him yet to our ways here. Please accept his big city apology, Cheryl." He turned to Trace. "Cab's waiting. See you tomorrow, Cheryl. Have a great evening." He tucked the box into his coat pocket and headed for the door leaving Trace no choice but to follow.

In the cab, Wayne handed the box back to Trace. "It's an insult to turn down a gift. Cheryl's uncle makes these for her and she gives them to few. Crew members who come in - are personable, cheerful and respectful of and with everyone. To receive one of these is an honor – and a privilege. It's her way of showing gratitude – friendship – kinship of a sort. It doesn't require a return gift. She didn't give it to receive anything in return – other than what you have already given."

"How do I apologize?" Trace asked as he tucked the box into his own pocket.

"You'll figure it out. Hey driver, can we have another cab here in about half an hour?" The cab turned into the parking lot at the Inlet Tower and stopped at the front door. While Wayne took care of the cab fare, Trace went inside to begin checking in. Wayne stopped, picked up his key and looked at the desk clerk. "Wake up call at 6:30? Let's move, Trace, we have a cab coming back."

In the elevator, Trace checked his watch; calculating time and decided that he could make a quick call to Lee before meeting Wayne downstairs. He hurried to his room, dropped his bag, grabbed the phone and dialed Lee's number. She answered on the fourth ring. "Lee, is everything OK?"

"Yes. I was just getting ready for bed."

"Aren't you up late?"

"I had some things to do. I'm going in late tomorrow. Where are you?"

"Anchorage. We got in a little over an hour ago, but there's always paperwork at Ops. We just got into the hotel. Wayne and I are going downtown to the Crow's Nest for dinner. It's a great place and has a fantastic view of the downtown area and out over Cook Inlet. I miss you and I wish you were here. I haven't time to talk more, Wayne ordered the cab back soon and I just dropped my bags and called you and I want to wash up before leaving."

"Go. Enjoy dinner. Call me in the morning. I love you."

Trace washed up and hurried back downstairs. Wayne was just getting into the cab. They chatted work as the cab sped toward the downtown area and pulled up at the Captain Cook. As they walked in, Trace noticed that the gift shop was still open.

"Wayne, go on up and get us a table. I'll be right up." He said as he turned toward the gift shop. There were several people in the shop and the lady behind the counter was intent on helping them which left Trace time to gaze about the well stocked store. There were shelves of stuffed animals, racks of colored t-shirts, shelves of china and glass and clayware, dolls in native costume, key chains, knick knacks, wall décor of birch bark, wood, metal, bone and fur. There were displays of ivory, baleen and soap stone. Trace picked up a stuffed polar bear, fingering the soft plush fur and still holding it, he walked to the counter to gaze at the displays of jewelry in the lighted glass case. By this time, the other customers had either gone or stepped back to discuss options and the lady behind the counter smiled as she approached him. "Is there something I can show you?" She asked.

Trace's eyes swept the selections, skipping over items that did not immediately catch his attention. He was about to shake his head in the negative when he noticed a necklace set back from the front of the glass. "That one." He said indicating his choice.

The attendant opened the case and pointed to one or two before placing her finger on the item that had caught Trace's attention. She placed it gently on the glass counter top. "A very nice piece." She said. "The beads are walrus ivory and gold." Small gold beads spaced the ivory beads in a single strand and in a waterfall cascade that tapered at the center. At the tip of each strand was a small, glistening ice blue tear shaped crystal. The lady tilted the box to show the price, looking up questioningly.

Trace nodded. "I'll take it."

"Certainly." The lady said. "Would you like it gift wrapped?"

"Not if you don't have a nice box." Trace answered.

"I'll be right back." She replied and turned away. When she returned, she opened the black velvet case she held. "Will this work?" The necklace lay in stunning contrast in the black velvet lined box she held out for Trace to examine.

"Perfect." Trace laid his credit card on the counter and set the bear down.

Ten minutes later, Wayne looked up as Trace sat down, placing the gift shop bag on the chair next to his own. "I took the liberty of ordering you a glass of wine. Merlot wasn't it? And I ordered some stuffed mushrooms and artichoke hearts. Looks as if the shopping trip was a success."

The waitress arrived with two glasses of wine. "Are you ready to order, gentlemen?" She asked.

Trace picked up the menu and glanced quickly down the selections. "I think I want the salmon, mashed potatoes and green beans with a side of salad with blue cheese, please."

"Good choice." She smiled as she made notes on her pad and then turned her attention to Wayne.

"The salmon is always a good choice." He echoed. "I think I'll take it, too, but I want garlic mashed potatoes and the spring greens peas in sauce and a salad with house dressing."

The waitress finished with a flourish, tucked the pad into a pocket of her apron, picked up the menus, smiled at both men and hurried away.

Wayne had chosen a window table that looked out over Cook Inlet where the landing lights of two aircraft probed the dusky night sky.

"That dark shadow way over there; the long, low hill; is called the Sleeping Lady." Wayne said as he sipped his wine.

"The Sleeping Lady?"

"Mount Susitna. It's a local legend. Two tribes were at war and it was bitter fighting that didn't show much chance of coming to a stop. One young warrior decided to approach the opposite tribe – alone – as an emissary of peace to talk them into stopping before both tribes were completely destroyed. He promised the girl he was to marry that he would return shortly. She missed him when he left and vowed to lie down and sleep until he returned. He was killed and she remains sleeping – awaiting the return of her warrior."

"A beautiful story. Cheryl tell you that one?"

The first time I heard it was from Jack Sterling – the first pilot I came in here with. It was in early summer – near midnight and the sun was still blazing bright in the blue sky and the Sleeping Lady was a dark image on the horizon as we came in. It is a uniquely shaped hill and it catches your attention.

An old native man sitting in Resolution Park in the setting sun later that fall told pretty much the same story. He said they were giants, people much bigger than live here today, but they fought terrible battles and killed until none were left. He said that when the warrior left the village he was gone a long time and the maiden worked each day waiting for him, unable to sleep with worry at night and when she finally slept, word arrived of the warrior's death and the people did not want to waken her from such peaceful sleep. So they left her and the battle came to them while she slept and more died until none were left. The sky was a dark pink above the Lady while he talked in his soft native way and rain clouds were hazy in the distance. Gold sparkled across the surface of the Inlet and the distant hills were faded blue against the sky line. He also said that this country always brings its' own home. I heard another version of the story from a lady in a local book store the next year. Though the minute details of the stories may vary, the basic line remains the same. There was war, there was a young man and a young woman in love, separated by war and then death and she waits his return. Is it not the story of every war?"

Trace looked out over the waters of the inlet, studying the supine figure of the woman that was the mountain. His thoughts slipped back to the slopes of Ghost Cave Mountain and the people who had once lived there. He thought of the young woman near the base of the mountain who must even now be getting ready to lie down, alone, waiting and he was caught short by the urgent need to return that coursed through his own body. His hand shook slightly as he lifted his glass and sipped wine.

"I'd like to go shopping before we leave tomorrow." He said as he moved aside his napkin and silverware to allow the waitress room to set down a basket of warm bread and butter.

Wayne picked up the two small plates and handed one to Trace. "What is it you need? Groceries? There's a small mart across the street from the Tower. There's a couple of large grocery stores, but not close enough to walk. There are malls, but again not walking distance. The closest would probably be the one on Benson where Sears is. I don't know if the courtesy van would take you there, but there are always cabs at the hotel. We're due out at 1:45 in the afternoon, but we should be at Ops about noon."

The waitress arrived with more food, offering more wine which they both declined in favor of coffee. Talk turned to work until the meal was cleared away.

"I hate to see you move on, Trace. I've enjoyed the time we worked together. But I understand the needs of life and I wish you the best. If I can help in any way, let me know."

"I haven't really had time to look at all my options. I think we run some flights out of Spokane and some out of Boise, but I haven't really looked at them yet because I know where I stand on the list. I was thinking of looking at the Forrest Service or BLM to see if they had any slots over there."

"I heard they're always looking for good crews. I have some connections up higher. Let me see what I can find out for you."

They paid the bill, caught the elevator down and stepped into the crisp evening air to hail a cab. A light snow had begun to fall and the cab slid a bit as it came in to the curb.

Back at the hotel, Trace turned on the television and listened to the news as he scanned the phone book for shops in the near vicinity. He made a couple of quick notes before turning the television and the lights out and slipped into bed. The nights since leaving Lee had been achingly empty and lonely – he missed her more now than he had before and he knew he would have to find a solution to their separation soon. He fell asleep thinking of Lee, remembering the warmth of her body next to his own, the softness of her skin.

The alarm broke through his sleep and he rolled to turn on the bedside lamp. Street light edged the window where the curtain gapped a bit. He turned off the alarm, rolled over and stretched before kicking aside the covers and padding softly to the window. Snow was drifting lazily from the sky, tumbling in the light of the street lamps. A few cars moved by on Minnesota Drive, moving slowly in the fresh snow accumulation on the surface of the street.

Trace moved back to drop down on the edge of the bed and reach for the phone. He dialed Lee's number and she answered on the third ring.

"Hello. Lee."

"Trace! Good morning. Did you have a good dinner?"

"And a history lesson. Wayne has been doing this so long he makes a good tour guide! We're out of here this afternoon. I'll be back home this evening. It's snowing here. And, God, but I miss you so much!!"

Lee laughed. "I'm glad to hear that Mr. Horn. I'd be disappointed if it were any different." Her voice dropped a bit and the tone took on a sadness. "I miss you, too, Trace. I can't wait for us to be together."

"It'll happen, honey. And then you'll be begging me to go away because I'll be such a pest. Underfoot all the time. Begging for attention."

"There you'll have to stand in line, you know. There's the baby….and mother…and my job…and all the other men in my life."

"As long as you save a spot somewhere in there for me. I'll just take the next available number!! Speaking of baby – have you chosen a name yet?"

"I've been giving it some thought over the months. Is there something you like? We can throw some options on the table, think about them and make a decision."

"If it's a girl, can we call her Lee?"

"No! But I thought Abilene might be cool….or maybe George."

"Lee! You wouldn't! A girl named George?"

"There was one in Nancy Drew. Her best friends were George and Bess. And both of them were girls."

"I bet it was short for Georgina."

"It never said that anywhere in any of the books I ever remember reading."

"Lee? You're joshing me aren't you? I mean about naming her George?"

Lee laughed. "I was trying to think of a way to name her after you and I can only come up with Tracey. Do you like that?"

"I think Tracey Lee would be a great name for her. But what if it's a boy?"

"I'd like the middle name to be Andrew after my dad."

"How about Turner Andrew?"

"Turner?"

"My grandfather." Trace said softly.

"Then Turner Andrew it is." Lee said quickly. "I waited for your call, but I have to get to work. I have to go. I miss you and can't wait to hear from you again."

"I love you more, Sweetheart. Talk to you tonight." Trace hung up, stood and stretched, then headed for the shower as he went back over the conversation. Just as he was about to step into the cascade of water, he stopped. He could have sworn he heard his grandfather's voice whispering. He shook his head. Only the hiss of the water, he thought and reached for the shampoo.

An hour later, he was ordering sourdough pancakes, bacon and eggs. He had bought a paper to read, but the words blurred and he saw the same words he had heard as he had stepped into the shower. He set the paper aside and watched the waitress as she worked the other tables, trying to focus on something more concrete than whispers from nowhere. But the words echoed through his thoughts as he searched jewelry store after jewelry store that morning.

On the way back to the hotel, empty handed, he gazed out of the cab window with a sense of sadness tugging at his heart. He wasn't sure what it was he was looking for, but though he had seen many beautiful sets, the right one was not among them. The cab stopped at a red light and Trace's eyes swept the buildings along the street. A narrow front jewelry store caught his attention and without thinking, he threw a twenty dollar bill on the front seat. "Circle a few times. I'll be right back." He said as he opened the door and all but jumped out of the car. A small bell tinkled as he opened the door of the jewelry shop. There were only a couple of display cases along either side of the room. A door opened to a back room where work benches were piled with clutters of boxes, tools and lamps. A tall, thin man with hollow cheeks and sparkling deep blue eyes stepped out of the back room. "I was beginning to think you would not come back." He said as he set a white velvet box on the counter top. "I believe this is what you wanted?"

"Come back?" Trace asked. "I don't believe I've been in here before."

"Oh, you were here last fall." The man replied. "I never forget a face. Or a special request." He pushed the box forward and Trace reached out to pick it up. He opened the top and looked at the ring set nestled in white velvet. A narrow rose gold wedding band with a row of 7 tiny diamonds down the center and an engagement ring of rose gold. A row of tiny diamonds swirled along the top of the band and at the center of the swirl raised up on a base of white gold, was a single brilliant ice blue diamond. He tipped the box and light flashed from the blue diamond.

"This is beautiful and exactly what I would have purchased if I had seen it. But I truly have never seen this before and someone will be disappointed to come back and find it gone."

"It was made to your design request." The man said. "I hope it's everything you expected and wanted it to be."

"But…" Trace started to speak, but the man reached into his shirt pocket and withdrew a small brown envelope and set it down on the counter.

"This is you?" The man said more than asked. On the surface of the envelope was 'T. L. Horn.'

Trace shook his head. He had never been in this store before. He had never seen this man before. But the set was perfect and he knew it. "That is my name and initials, but truly, sir, I have never been in this store before today. May I ask how much this set would cost?" He asked.

The man turned the envelope over. "$675.00 is the remaining balance. I couldn't sell it to anyone else since you have paid so much already for it and it was a special design, made exclusively for you Mr. Horn."

"Remaining?" Trace asked puzzled. "I think there is some mistake here. I can't take something that someone else has paid for and is expecting to

217

find when they come back. Surely the full price was much higher."

The man sighed. "I can't keep the piece, Mr. Little Horn. Not after you paid so much for it."

Trace was stunned. How could this man know his name? Until Lee, he had only introduced himself as Trace Horn. He pulled out his wallet, set three one hundred dollar bills on the counter and set his credit card on top. Less than five minutes had passed when he stepped back onto the street to find the cab just pulling up along the curb. He tucked the white velvet box into his pocket, slid into the back seat of the cab and directed the driver to the Inlet Tower, his thoughts tumbling over the events in the jewelry shop.

He hurried up to his room, made one last scan of the room to make sure he had everything and lifted his bag off the bed. Wayne's voice came with the knock on the door and the door opened.

"Trace?"

"Yeah. I'm ready." He turned to follow his fellow pilot out of the room.

"It's snowing again." Wayne said as he stepped into the small elevator that rattled noisily downward. "I'd like to see if we can take off early. Any luck shopping today?"

"Wasn't snowing when I arrived a few minutes ago." Trace replied. "I had an odd experience this morning though."

"Odd?" Wayne asked as they stepped out of the elevator and walked across the narrow lobby to the door.

A cab was pulled up at the curb. Wayne opened the back door and slid across the seat allowing Trace to slip in. Huge, fluffy snowflakes drifted lazily out of the leaden gray skies and visibility was already beginning to diminish.

"Winter just doesn't want to let go." The cab driver commented. "This wasn't in the forecast for today. By the look of the sky across the Inlet I'd say it's gonna get a lot thicker before the afternoon is over." He turned left onto Minnesota Drive and then swerved hard left against the curb as a car coming off 12th Avenue, slid into the intersection.

Both pilots were brushing snow off their shoulders and arms as they stepped into Ops less than fifteen minutes later. Cheryl laughed and shook her head. "You got here just in time. We just moved up your departure time. Fuel truck is already out on the pad and the de-icing crew is on standby. I just made fresh coffee. Better get a cup while you can."

"I'll get the coffee and take our stuff out while you get the rest of the paperwork and latest weather." Trace offered.

Half an hour later they were taxiing to the end of the runway. A gentle breeze slanted the falling snow and swirled it about on the ground further reducing the already low visibility. An incoming passenger plane created a wall of white as it touched down. A few minutes after it cleared away, the tower gave Wayne clearance for take-off. As they picked up speed for lift off, snow swirled, spreading out like giant wings on each side and fanning out into a billowing cloud behind them. They lifted off into a blanket of fluffy clouds that enveloped the aircraft almost instantly, blocking off visual sight of the land below them. Dusk fell in the cockpit, but both men were busy with take-off tasks, watching instruments and making small adjustments as they climbed higher into the thickening cloud bank. They were well out over the coastal waters before they broke out of the clouds and leveled out. With all the instruments and the autopilot set, both men leaned back. Trace poured two cups of coffee from the thermos he had filled in Ops.

Wayne took his cup, glanced out at the wisps of cloud they were skimming. "You had an interesting morning, you said earlier."

"I had an odd experience." Trace corrected. "I stopped in a small jewelry store and the man who waited on me said that I had been in the store last fall and had my order ready."

"Last fall?"

"Yes."

"A little past fall, but I suppose he might refer to it as fall."

"I suppose, but I don't recall ever being in that store before this morning and surely I would remember especially if I put in an order for a special purchase and I wasn't even thinking along those lines until a month ago."

"What lines?"

"Getting married. I had no plan in November of getting married. Lee and I didn't discuss it til Christmas."

"So you went into the store on your first trip up here and ordered something made?"

"Wayne. Every trip up here has left little to no time for any type of shopping other than the grocery or mall. He said I ordered a wedding and engagement ring set – special design. Lee and I weren't even talking in November. I met her last summer. I didn't think she would be interested in me or my life style and I left rather abruptly. I never could get her out of my mind. I kept going over everything that happened between us again and again. A lot of it didn't make sense. Then I realized that I had projected things from my past into our brief relationship without any idea as to whether they were valid. I had to see her, talk to her and see if there was any basis to the relationship or my actions. It wasn't until then – Christmas – that we worked things out and decided that we cared about each other. She felt the same way I did. The idea of looking for a wedding set here only came after we landed the other day. When we checked into the hotel, I noticed the wedding ring the desk manager was wearing. I liked the gold and the setting and I asked questions. It was then I decided to look here for something special, something I might not be able to find in Seattle."

"So you fell for his line? Did you buy the set? Are you sure the place is legit?"

"I can't say I 'fell' for his line. The set is stunning and real. But he came out of the back room when I came in and he had an envelope that had 'T. L. Horn' written on it. The set was in the envelope."

"Well, there may be someone with those initials and last name and they may have looked vaguely like you. If the man only came in once and several months ago, he may have assumed it was you."

"That was my thought line. I tried to tell him I hadn't been in and I hadn't ordered anything. Then he addressed me by my full name which I had not mentioned and I never tell anyone."

"You mean your name really isn't Trace Horn?"

"Oh, it is. But that's the abbreviated name I use. He knew the whole name."

"Abbreviated?"

"It's a long story, Wayne and my own tale of woe and maybe someday I'll tell you the story. I don't use my entire name because of...well...things that happened. It's not that I change my name. My whole name is on legal documents, I just don't use it in everyday associations. I found sometimes it was easier that way. So I was really thrown for a loop when he used the entire form of my name. It is not common. I couldn't refute that I am who I am. And I couldn't convince him that I had never been in before. Someone who looks pretty much like me, I can buy. Even someone with a name close to mine, I can buy. But both with one person is a pretty far pull from a total stranger."

"Yeah, I suppose. Was this set expensive?"

"Well, that's the other thing. He said that I had already paid the larger amount of the bill and what was left was very minimal for the quality of what he showed me. I tried to protest again and that was when he called me by my full name."

"You didn't take it, did you?"

"What would you have done?"

"I'd have told him there was some kind of mistake."

"I tried that. But you see, Wayne, my whole name is an Indian name. And I know there are native's here in Alaska, but their last names are way different than those in the Lower 48."

"Ah, so now we're getting down to some hard facts here! I was beginning to think that you would beat around the bush all afternoon! You must be hedging around the fact that you're Native American?"

"I've never outright denied it. I just never mention it, nor do I allow my name to introduce it. I don't want to be judged for my heritage. I want to be judged for who I am."

"There are some in this world, Trace, who don't see much of anything. There are a good number of people who have the look, may even have the bloodline, but have no knowledge of it. That you are Native American makes no difference to me. A good number of Americans have a little of it in their blood anyway, a lot so diluted that you could never believe it's there. It's no mark of shame nor should you allow anyone to make you think it is."

"That's easy to say if you haven't walked the path I have, Wayne, but I appreciate the vote of confidence and I thank you. But, yes, it has proven to be a challenge…and a barrier at times in my life."

"It couldn't have mattered to the company or they wouldn't have hired you. Before I met you, I was told only that according to your military records you were one qualified pilot. You came highly recommended by your last employer and you presented all of both back grounds in your interview in such a manner that he was impressed enough to hire you. And in the time I've worked with you, I'd say he made a right good decision in doing so. Now that we have that settled, what does that have to do with what happened this morning?"

"Only the man's knowledge of my whole name."

"A lucky guess?"

"I hardly think so. I always sign my name as Trace L. Horn. I introduce myself either as that or just plain Trace Horn. 'L' could stand for any number of names. You would have to know me to know that the 'L' stands for Little. And he called me Mr. Little Horn. But I have never been in that store. I have never seen that man and I never ordered the making of anything, but what he showed me was perfect and to make matters even odder, it matches the necklace that I bought at the hotel last night."

"There are a lot of odd coincidences in there, I have to admit. Care to show me the pieces?"

Trace pulled out the package with the necklace in it, opened the box and handed it to Wayne. Then he pulled out the second small box and handed it over. Wayne opened the small white velvet box, then looked quickly back at the necklace. He looked up at Trace.

"These look as if they were all made to order as a matching set. You bought them in two different places? As long as I've been coming up here I don't believe I've ever seen anything even close to this. And yet you have two pieces, bought from different places, that could be easily seen as an entire matched set. That and everything else is really odd. Not sure I understand the how or why of it."

"Not sure I do either. But my grandfather taught me that life is a fabric made up of people, animals, things and events that come into our lives with reason and purpose. Threads flow through life connecting and weaving all life together. Cheryl is a Native Alaskan. She has an uncle who makes ivory carvings. I fly and so do you. Cheryl gives me an ivory aircraft which connects all of us. But it is given to me when I fly with you. Then when we go out for dinner I find the ivory and blue crystal necklace. Next day I find a gold and blue diamond ring set. A circle has been formed. But where did the ring set come from? Who ordered it? Who paid for it? Who is the other T. Little Horn? And why does he look so much like me? How did I find that jewelry shop? Why did I choose to go in? What are the chances of all of that happening? Why do all these things seem to be connected?"

Wayne laughed. "The way you say it, it does sound like one heck of a mystery! You're gonna make me believe in strange things you keep talking like that!"

"Well, add a few more things to the list. Lee lives at the foot of a mountain known as Ghost Cave Mountain. It was the mountain where my grandfather was raised and her father was lost. It's where I met Lee. And since I visited that mountain last summer, I can almost feel my grandfather around me sometimes."

Wayne was silent for a few moments, sipping coffee, glancing across the banks of instruments. When he spoke again his voice was low, hesitant. "I believe, Trace, sometimes, that there are people on this earth who are closer to God and heaven than most others. I believe sometimes that the Native Americans have a better understanding of this natural world than we do and that their religion connected them; grounded them to it in a much deeper, open and purer manner than most people can ever imagine and few get close to in their own beliefs. No people have ever understood their priests, or shamans or wise men. They were always feared even if they were respected simply because they walked and talked closer to God than the rest of us. I don't know what's right or wrong in that field, and I don't think most others do either. We just cling as close to faith as we can and hope we have a measure of it right. If you're checkin to see if I think that makes you crazy, you're not gonna find it or hear it. How am I to judge what you see and feel when I can't see or feel what you do? How can I say it's right or wrong? True or false? I'd like to think the people I've loved and lost in this life are close enough to see and feel me even if I can't them. I'd like to think they care enough to check back once in awhile to kinda say 'hi' in the only fashion they can now. I think we have angels, guardians, who help us, whether we know it or not, believe it or not. If there are angels that are putting the pieces together and tugging the strings to put you and Lee together, then there must be some high good in your being there. If they're laying out crumbs on the path cause you're too blind to see what's in front of your face, it's because they care enough to make sure you find the right path. I'd call that pretty special. I'd say you had some people in your life once that loved you a whole lot and I don't believe they've stopped that or wanting what's best for you, what would make you happiest."

The cabin darkened as they entered a high cloud bank and neither man spoke. Both sipped coffee. Both lost in thoughts. In their own worlds and life events that had somehow been shadowed by the path of conversation. Memories of other people, other times glimmered on the edge of emotion.

I don't remember my grandfather…either one." Wayne said softly. "Sounds like you were close to yours."

"My father's father. I never knew my father. He was killed in Viet Nam when I was very small. My mother remarried a couple of years later and my step father just couldn't accept me, so mother sent me to live with my father's family. My grandfather was more than a grandfather. He was the only father I ever knew. He was my closest and best friend. Sometimes I feel his presence as if he were right beside me, but that's not surprising as close as we were. Sometimes I wish I could sit down and talk to him, share what's going on in life. Listen to his words and sort out what he's saying to me in a manner that I have to find my own answers in them. He never told me what to do when I came to him with a problem. He told a story and left me and I sorted through the story until I figured out what he was telling me, what lesson there was in it. I think it was the way he was raised. He was very quiet and spiritual in a deep and silent way, a devoted family man. He was my model. Sometimes I don't think I walk well in his path."

Wayne smiled. "I think you do a fine job. I think he'd be very proud of what you've achieved in your life. Don't be so hard on yourself. Don't let the world hold you down because they don't understand who you are. You don't owe that to the world or anyone else. There's a lot about you that reminds me of Cheryl. Quiet. Watching life and those in it. Learning and giving in a quiet way that few see or understand. I think that's why she likes you. She sees into your heart."

"It was the way of the old people. Few know those ways. Everyone in too big of a hurry to make it to the head of the line. Be the most important one there."

Again they fell silent. Outside, droplets of water accumulated to run in streams down the windshield. Clouds wrapped around the aircraft like a blanket. Inside, lights on the dash lit up the cabin with soft light. The radio was silent.

"What would you think if you were in my shoes?" Trace asked softly.

Wayne sipped his coffee and scanned the instruments, before looking over at Trace. "I don't know. I guess I'd do what you're doing."

"Wayne, would you be interested in standing up with me when Lee and I get married?"

Wayne chuckled. "Wouldn't miss it for the world, my friend. Finish that coffee, Seattle will be on to us in less than five minutes and I want all of your attention to getting this bird on the deck."

*****

January passed quickly. Seattle weather held mostly to heavy overcast often with drizzling rain and some wind. Anchorage held to temperatures hovering below freezing. Neither location encouraged much adventuring out to explore. Trace fell into a routine that passed the time quickly. Wayne had done some research into job positions for him and Trace made contacts and filled out applications and paperwork. He called Lee frequently, and they planned the small Valentine wedding. Trace had requested and been given eight days off spanning the middle of the month. He was planning to drive over on the Saturday before the 14th. Wayne and his wife were planning on driving over two days later to meet them in Sand Point.

Friday morning, fog lay heavy over all of Anchorage and flights were delayed as the temperature hung below seasonal norms. Wayne and Trace left the Inlet Towers late due to the delays and then sat in operations waiting for a break. Cheryl arrived late and cranky because her car had not started and traffic had been snail slow in the near zero visibility. She hung up her coat and turned to look at Trace.

"Are you ready to go to Idaho? I was watching the news while I was getting dressed this morning and the passes out of Seattle are closed due to storms."

"They should have them clear by tomorrow." Trace replied. "I'm not leaving until tomorrow morning."

229

Cheryl glanced out of the window at the fog swirling around the building and then began collecting papers from the fax machine. "Best make a flight reservation. You'll need it."

Wayne raised an eyebrow as he poured another cup of coffee and looked over at Trace near the window. "Is she implying that we're not getting out of here or you won't drive out of Seattle?"

Trace turned to reply, but the phone rang and Cheryl lifted her hand at the two men. When she hung up, she put a packet of papers together. "Take these. The tower wants us ready, so best get out to the plane. Trace, make that reservation as soon as you get a chance."

An hour later, they lifted off the runway in swirling tendrils of fog that gave occasional glimpses of snow covered terrain. As they gained altitude, the fog gave way to thick clouds that wrapped around the aircraft, enveloping it in a dark duskiness while the instrument panel provided the only dim colored light in the cabin. They kept climbing and gradually the clouds gave way to thin tufts until they broke out above. The sun was dropping toward the horizon while soft hues of lavender and gold touched the tops of the clouds and tinged the icy blue of the sky. As far as the eye could see, a blanket of multi-hued clouds hid the world from sight. And it remained so all the way to Seattle. They dropped through the clouds, into darker thickness and then broke out just above the city in pouring rain.

Trace completed the onboard paperwork while Wayne went into Ops. When Trace arrived, Wayne was waiting. "You have an emergency call, Trace.

From Idaho. They've been trying to get word to us all day."

Trace felt the color drain from his face as he hurried into the office. Dan Folgers, the Operations Manager, stood up as he entered the office. "Trace, we've been trying all day to get a hold of you. We got a call this morning. You can use my phone. Call this number." And he handed Trace a small piece of paper.

Trace felt his hand trembling as he punched in the numbers. A woman answered, identifying the hospital. Trace could only think of Lee. "Is Lee McDougal there?"

"One moment please."

The second hand on the wall clock clicked by the seconds until another voice answered. Once again, Trace could only ask for Lee.

"One moment, please."

More seconds and then another voice. "Hello?"

"Lee McDougall?" Trace asked.

"Oh, yes. Are you Trace Little Horn?"

"Yes. Is Lee OK?"

"Yes, she's fine. She started labor about 4 this morning. She's doing fine."

"But she's not due for another month. What happened? Is everything all right?"

"The doctor's not here right now, but I can let you speak to Miss McDougall for a moment. Let me transfer the call to her room."

Seconds. And then Lee's voice. "Hello?"

"Lee! What happened? Are you all right?"

"I'm fine – just in labor and it hurts. Pains started about 4 this morning. I called the hospital at 7 and went in about 9. I came to Sand Point by ambulance and got in about 3. The doctor's been in a couple of times. This is early. There doesn't seem to be anything really wrong. My water hasn't broken yet. They're monitoring the baby close and so far everything seems to be going well. But I don't think it's going to wait for you to drive over."

"I'll get a flight and be there as soon as I can."

Trace hung up and explained to Dan and Wayne what was going on.

All of the evening flights were full. Wayne made a couple of phone calls and then turned to Trace. "I can get a charter to leave in just over half an hour. Just enough time to get you over to Boeing Field. There isn't time to get your truck, you'll have to take a cab. Your truck will be OK here and if you want I can pick some things up from your place and bring over."

Trace gave Wayne the key to his apartment. "My bag is packed. In my room. Appreciate it."

Fifteen minutes later he was in a cab on his way to Boeing Field. The windshield wipers beat a steady rhythm against a torrent of rain water. Traffic on I-5 was slow – a combination of the hour and the weather. The cab slipped across lanes, dodging in between vehicles before finally making the exit off the busy freeway. As they pulled into the flight area they had been directed to, Trace could see an aircraft taxiing into place. He handed two twenty dollar bills to the cab driver. "Keep the change." He said as he jumped out and reached for his bags. He dashed through the downpour, splashing through puddles of water to the door. Inside, the room was almost over bright after the subdued tones of darkness and heavy rain outside. Trace set down his bags and turned to the counter. A young woman with bright purple hair snapped gum as she watched him approach.

"Kin ah hep you?" She drawled.

"Trace Little Horn. I just arranged for a charter."

"Mmm." She moved some papers around snapping gum noisily. "Had a call fer a charter, but not a Little Horn."

"No, that would have been Wayne Gardner. He made the calls for me."

"Mmmhmm. Be a bit. He's just pullin in. Some coffee over there on the table. Kinda old, but it's warm." She turned away and stepped into a small office.

Trace glanced at the coffee and decided against it. He dropped his bags on a bench and brushed at the water clinging to his jacket.

"Trace Little Horn?"

Trace turned. A man had stepped out of the same office the young woman had disappeared into. Broad shouldered, muscular, thick wavy brown hair that fell over his forehead and laughing green eyes set into a leathery tanned face. He looked like a television commercial ad cowboy, but Trace liked him immediately.

"Yes."

The man wiped his hands on a faded gray towel and reached out to shake. "Slade Masters. Known Wayne fer a lot a years. You ready?"

"Yes."

"Good. Them yer bags?" Before Trace could reply, Slade stepped past him and lifted the larger of the two bags. Trace picked up his flight bag and followed Slade around the corner and through the back office. They stepped outside, back into the torrential downpour and all but ran for the waiting aircraft.

Slade leaped up the steps easily, dropped Trace's bag and turned as Trace ducked into the cabin. "Go ahead and take the right seat while I secure these bags in the cargo net." He said as he reached for the bag Trace held.

Five minutes later, he slid into the left seat and reached for a clipboard to finish paperwork. "This storm hit in the early morning hours last night and dumped a good amount of snow in the mountains. The passes were closed until early afternoon. This rain started heavy about mid-afternoon and should be letting up in the next hour, but we'll be flying out of it as we head east." Trace nodded and watched the ground crew pull away the steps and stand by to pull the wheel chocks. Slade finished, set aside the clipboard, scanned the instruments, glanced out the window and gave a thumbs up to the ground crew. The wheel chocks were pulled and the ground crew stepped clear as Slade applied throttle and the engine roared to prepare for taxi. They rolled slowly at first, Slade adjusting settings and calling the tower for takeoff instructions. The aircraft picked up momentum as it hurled down the runway and then lifted into the air as the clouds thinned and the lights of the city glowed in the darkness below. The aircraft skimmed out over the Duwamish River and banked over Elliott Bay, turning east, crossing over a trail of moving red lights that marked I-5 below them. As they flew further east and gained altitude, the clouds thinned showing a thin trace of moonlight now and then.

Slade remained silent until they had crossed over the mountains. Then he set the autopilot and reached for a thermos to pour coffee, handing the first cup to Trace. "We have a bit of easy flight time. Might just as well relax and enjoy the ride while we can. You been flying with Wayne awhile?"

"Just about six months."

"Great guy. We met several years ago, both of us flying out of Boise. We may run into some heavy clouds half way between Moses Lake and Spokane. There's a snow storm coming down out of Canada, but we should be able to make Sand Point before it drops down too hard. We should be on the ground there by midnight."

Trace glanced at his watch. It had been nearly two hours since he had talked to Lee. He closed his eyes and sent out a silent prayer that things were going well and he would make it in before delivery. Then he turned his attention back to the scene outside as he sipped more coffee. His thoughts drifting, his attention not focused on any one thing, his eyes scanning the sky, the dark drifting clouds, the moonlight penetrating the thinner layers and outlining columns and tufts. Now and then a white expanse below, cold and distant. A shape took form against the drifting clouds, wavering and faint, but as moonlight backlit the form he heard the voice reaching out to him. "Turner Cassidy." Trace turned quickly to see if Slade had heard, but he was watching the instruments and when Trace turned back to the window, the image was gone. He shook his head. He was tired and stressed. He set down the coffee mug, rubbed his eyes and stretched.

"Tired?" Slade asked.

"Yes and no. I guess. Up early in Anchorage. Weather delays. Long flight back to Seattle. And now this. Waiting. Not knowing."

"First?"

"Yes."

"They say you can get that way. I've seen some guys just carry on like nothing was new. Don't know as how I'd handle it myself."

"You don't have kids?"

"Not even married. Came close once, but she got cold feet thinkin about bein married to a pilot I guess."

"No one serious?"

"Not really. I see several girls. No one special. One in Portland. A couple in Seattle. One in Moses Lake and one in Bellingham. I like the freedom of being able to do things when I'm gone and I'm gone a lot. I don't view them as girlfriends. They're just friends I like and like to do things with. No strings. No ties."

The radio came to life and they listened to the voices of other pilots and the tower at Moses Lake.

The ground slipped by below, the moon slipped in and out among the clouds, the clouds changed shape and form and density continually around them in an ever moving kaleidoscope of night shades and formations. Then a thin arc of light appeared on the distant horizon.

"That will be Spokane." Slade said quietly.

Before they arrived over Spokane, a wind began to buffet the aircraft, tossing it gently to and fro. As they began to descend on approach to Sand Point, the wind hurled huge flakes of soft snow at them that became a thick curtain as they continued downward. The runway appeared suddenly out of the swirling mass and Slade touched the wheels gently to the surface. The aircraft skipped and bounced, then settled onto the tarmac and began to slow.

Slade opened the door and a gust of wind swept a cold blast of air into the warm interior. Trace pulled his jacket on, grasped his flight bag and followed Slade as the ground crew pushed steps into place. The two men dashed across the windswept tarmac to the building, ducking their heads as the wind kicked up snow and swirled it about. The door banged open, warm air met cold and formed a cloud of moisture laden air that drifted and dissipated in the room.

"You just made it in time." A slender dark haired woman greeted them. "This storm is picking up some backbone. They were just talking about shutting down the field if this wind and snow come in any stronger. Slade, it's good to see you, again. You don't come over enough and all of us girls miss you! You gonna stick around a day or so or are you skedaddling before they shut us down? If you're stayin, I gotta call my husband and tell him I won't be home tonight!"

"Mary, you know that Mike will only laugh and ask you to pick up more beer for company. How is he anyway? Still wrestling trucks at the fire station?"

"Yep. He talks about retiring, but I just don't see him doing that. Jr. moved back last summer and is working out of the fire base. He's married now and they have two little girls."

Slade wrapped his arms around the dark haired beauty and kissed the top of her head. "And I bet gramma is in seventh heaven with two more to spoil. How are the other two?"

Megan's girls are growing like bad weeds. Jenny just turned seven and Donna will be five next month. And they both look just like their mama. Good thing. That no account Tommy is still an ugly truck driver!"

"Now! Now! Mary! You know you like him near as much as me. Hey, are any cabs running out here or can we get a rental car? My passenger here needs to get to the hospital as soon as possible."

"Everything closed down over an hour ago. We have the spare van. Where you guys stayin?"

"I'll probably stay at the Holiday. Don't know about him. Guess he'll figure that out later. Mind if I drop him off at the hospital? I'll clean up, pick up a six pack and meet you at the house. Want me to pick up pizza on the way?"

"Go ahead. Key's hanging on the rack in the back office. I'll call Mike and tell him to throw an extra steak on, he was just starting the grill when I talked to him a few minutes ago. Don't dally or your steak will be crisp!"

Snow plows and sanding trucks were not yet on the streets and snow was already creating difficult driving conditions. Wind drifted it across the road and streets, dimming the light of the street lamps. At the hospital, Trace jumped out into the brisk wind, pulling his collar up before he grabbed his bags, thanked Slade and turned to the door.

He stopped at the front desk, then hurried upstairs to stop at yet another desk. The hall was dim; doors closed or half closed; a hush in the air. The nurse at the desk smiled and came around to lead him down the hall. She stopped at a closed door, opened it and stepped aside. Trace stepped past her, set his bags down by the door, pushed aside the curtain and stepped into the room. Light was dim, sending reflections of the room off the large plate glass window as if it were a mirror. A large chair was pushed into a corner, up in the opposite corner a small TV screen glowed and, without sound, a couple spun in a graceful dance upon a glistening floor while curtains shimmered behind them. Monitors, and IV stands blocked access to the side of the bed which was set at an angle out of another corner. Lee lay silent, her eyes closed, the covers draped across her swollen body. A nurse adjusted an IV and scanned a narrow band of paper spewing from a monitor. She looked up. "Miss McDougal, I think you have company." She said softly.

Lee turned, opening her eyes and smiled weakly as she recognized Trace. She lifted her hand and he moved to the bedside and leaned over, taking her hand, brushing his lips across her cheek, then her lips. "Lee, honey, is everything OK? I've been so worried."

Suddenly, Lee tensed, closed her eyes and breathed in sharply. The nurse reached out, touched her arm and spoke soothingly. "Deep breaths. Easy. Try to relax, flow with it."

Lee shook her head, burrowed it deeper into the pillows and puffed breaths in and out, her grasp on Traces hand tightening. As the spasm eased, tears slid down her cheek and Trace brushed them away. She looked up at him. "My water broke about twenty minutes ago and the pains have gotten worse. The doctor's on his way down."

She had barely finished speaking when another contraction stopped her words. This time she lifted her head and shoulders.

The curtain swept aside as the doctor entered. "Push!" The nurse directed and the doctor moved around to take his position at the foot of the bed. Trace moved around the bed and once again took Lee's hand. The pain subsided and she dropped back against the pillows.

Trace was watched as nurses and doctor worked in unison with Lee; encouraging, coaching, soothing. "One more push." The doctor directed and suddenly he was holding a tiny form in his hands. "You have a son!" The doctor said quietly.

"Congratulations." The nurse echoed as she took the infant and handed him off to another nurse.

Trace was stunned at how tiny the infant was. He watched as the nurse took him and began cleaning his mouth and nose. The infant squirmed, caught his breath and let out a sudden small squeal. The nurse laughed. "OK. Now let's get you to the nursery, young man." She said as she set him into a glass infant crib and turned him away.

The doctor was directing Lee yet again when suddenly he looked up. "Keep pushing, Lee, I think we have a surprise here. Looks like we have a set of twins."

Two and half minutes later a second tiny form was handed off. "You have another son." The doctor confirmed.

Half an hour later, Lee was sleeping, the nurses had cleared the room of all equipment, the doctor was gone and Trace followed a nurse down the hall to the nursery. In a small room, a large glass enclosed infant crib sat with a curtain on three sides, monitors and dim lights. Two tiny boys, clad only in small diapers that were too large for them, lay side by side, arms and legs moving a bit now and then.

A doctor turned as Trace came in.

"Congratulations." He said. "I'm Doctor Morgan. Bit of a surprise, I hear." He said as he indicated the occupants of the crib. "It's not unusual for twins to be a month or so early. Usually we know they're coming and are a little more prepared. We have charts started. Have you decided on names so we can begin to separate the charts and data?"

"Turner Andrew was the only one we chose." So I guess he's the first one."

"The larger of the two." The doctor explained. He weighed four pounds, eight and a half ounces."

Trace hesitated. "Cascade John." He said softly. 'Turner Cascade.' He repeated under his breath. He smiled as he recalled the events of the past months.

"Cascade weighed in at four pounds, one ounce." The doctor went on. "They'll spend some time in these. Usually babies born early have to catch up, so to speak. Their lungs aren't usually fully ready to deal with the world and we have to keep a sharp eye for problems. You and Miss McDougal are encouraged to come in and spend as much time as possible with the boys. Hold them, cuddle them. They need lots of love and attention. The nurses here are dedicated to help and support you in any way they can. Feel free to ask them. The boys will only benefit from a unified effort to give them everything they need."

"Thank you." Trace said as moved closer. The doctor and nurse stepped aside to allow him to stand at the bedside. He reached in to touch first one tiny fist and then another. Emotions overwhelmed him as he looked down upon the two small boys – his sons. A combination of himself and Lee and he was torn by the memory that he had almost missed this. He brushed a tear away. "We are a family, boys. We gotta take care of your mamma. She needs you, too."

He returned to Lee's rooms, kissed her forehead, her cheeks, her lips while she slept. A nurse brought in blankets and pillows and opened up the chair into a bed. Trace pushed his bags into the corner beneath the TV, laid out the blankets and laid down. His eyes closed and he was asleep.

"Trace?" He opened his eyes. Lee stood by his side, her hair brushed, a pale blue robe wrapped around her shoulders.

Trace sat up, reaching for her hand.

"Look." She said.

Trace turned to the window. Snow was piled deeply all over the world outside. Sun touched the fresh drifts and sent brilliant sparkles into the crisp air. The sky above was a cool icy blue without a hint of clouds.

"I want to go to the nursery. And I don't want to go alone." Lee said.

Trace stood up, stretched, then slipped his arm around Lee's shoulder. They walked to the nursery. "Twins. I can't believe it. They're so tiny. And I think they're both going to look like their father. Look at all that black hair!" Lee whispered as she looked at the sleeping boys. "But Trace, we only picked one name."

"Turner Andrew was the first born." Trace told her. "Cascade John was two and a half minutes later."

Lee looked up at him. "Cascade John?"

"Turner Cascade was my grandfather's name. Cascade Turner was my father's. Andrew John was your father." Grandfather wanted the boys named after them all."

"Your grandfather?" Lee asked puzzled.

"It's a long story. And we have a life time to tell it. Those two boys are gonna be just fine. I know it. They have a couple of guardian angels who plan on making sure of that!"

Trace pulled Lee into his arms. "I love you more than words can ever say, Lee McDougal. And I can't wait to make you my wife next week. I'm looking forward to many years and a few more babies with you so get use to the idea that you can't get rid of me."

The curtain swayed. The boys turned their heads, kicked their legs and waved their arms about. Lee lifted her head from Trace's chest, sure that she had seen someone come to stand at his side, but they were alone. Trace had seen and felt, too. He tightened his arms, drawing Lee closer. "I love you, Lee McDougal." He whispered. 'And I love you, too, grandfather.' He thought.

**THE END**

# RETURN TO GHOST CAVE MOUNTAIN
to be released in the spring of 2013

Visit Alaska Dreams Publishing at
www.alaskadp.com

Karen J. Simon

# ABOUT THE AUTHOR

Originally from Eastern Montana, Karen moved to Alaska in early 1969 and with the exception of eight years spent in Seattle, she has called Alaska home.

She published her first poem in 1990 in the All Alaska Weekly. Two books of poetry and one of short stories followed. One poetry book and the short story are in the UAF library on the Fairbanks campus. She finds peace in painting the magnificent grandeur of Alaska's pristine wilderness bathed in the alpine glow of sunrise, radiant in the soft colors of sunset or breathtakingly beautiful as the Northern Lights arc the winter sky.

She has driven thousands of miles over Alaska roads from one end of the state to the other and worked all manner of jobs from retail clerk to cocktail waitress, construction crew to security officer, office manager to airline ramp, fashion model to tour bus driver and Safety/Compliance Supervisor for a major tour company.

A mother of two, she currently resides in Fairbanks with her granddaughter.

Karen J. Simon